I WILL
GO WITH
YOU

THE FLIGHT OF A LIFETIME

By Priya Kumar

Best selling author of: **'I AM ANOTHER YOU'**

COGNITE

I WILL GO WITH YOU

THE FLIGHT OF A LIFETIME

Published by:

COGNITE :
An Imprint Of Embassy Books
120, Great Western Building,
Maharashtra Chamber of Commerce Lane,
Fort, Mumbai 400 023,
India
Tel: 022-22819546 / 32967415
Email: info@embassybooks.in
www.embassybooks.in

Book design :Namrata Chattaraj

ISBN :978-93-83359-66-0

Printed & Bound in India by Repro India Ltd., Navi Mumbai

"It requires real strength to love Man. And to love him despite all invitations to do otherwise, all provocations and all reasons why one should not.

Happiness and strength endure only in the absence of hate. To hate alone is the road to disaster. To love is the road to strength. To love in spite of all is the secret of greatness. And may very well be the greatest secret in this universe."

....

L. RON HUBBARD

....

DEDICATION

I dedicate the book to the victims of the missing Malaysian Airlines who are still left with hollow hearts, haunted every night by thoughts of what could have happened or is happening to their loved ones who had boarded the flight MH370 on the fateful day of 8th March 2014.

In my perspective, real victims are the ones who are left behind in a state of helplessness, nursing fragmented hope, with wavering faith in the Almighty, when their loved ones go missing. Such is the fate of the families of the passengers aboard MH370; its missing status does not allow them to make peace with the death of their loved ones nor ease their heart that they still could be alive somewhere.

My aunt, Laaj Shahani, lost her husband in an air crash fifty-three years ago. They found the aircraft, but they never found his body. She would not believe that he was dead. She went to astrologers and soothsayers and when some told her that he was still alive, that he had lost his memory and that he would come back, she clutched that thread of hope and waited for him to return. She went to temples and priests and subjected her life to prayer for his return.

She never gave up hope for she could not believe that he was gone. Where was the evidence? Was it wrong to believe? Was it wrong to hope? Was it wrong to hold on to when she could feel his presence and his love? She waited for him to come back, everyday. It has been fifty-three years ever since.

If the plane had crashed at sea, the death could be palatable. But when a plane goes missing or when the plane is found at land and the body goes missing, the people left behind are victims forever; victims of their own imagination and their hopeless pleas to the gods with who their loved ones probably rest.

When closure is missing from life, every day seems like death.

I dedicate this book to all the people that hurt for being denied that loved one whom they don't know how to let go, for they still exist for them, only that they not there. I dedicate this book to my aunt, Laaj.

I hope that my book brings that closure to their pain, where the love can remain and the nightmares can end.

....

SONU NIGAM

....

Goodness flows where Sonu goes.

Your purpose and your passion humbles me. Knowing you has been a relief, for knowing that you are there, is also knowing that love, kindness, goodness and divinity will continue to persist.

Over the many years that I have known you, I have watched you unfailing hold a stand of sanity, courage and humanity. When negativity comes your way, it stops right there. It is never passed forward. Goodness finds its source in you. You have used your position to help others. You have used your power to uplift others. You have forwarded your talent, to serve, to contribute, and above all, to heal.

My admiration for you continues to grow beyond the bounds of words. Thank you for being who you are.

....

THANK YOU

....

I am glad that I still have a chance to appreciate and acknowledge all those who have contributed to my work, my happiness and my success.

As long as this book will endure, my gratitude for my mother will be known in written words. She is my biggest supporter. I wouldn't know what to do without her. I don't want to know either.

My brother Kapil, my sister-in-law Suchita, my nieces Aarya and Myra, are my greatest fans, or that is what I pretend to believe. Since they didn't bother reading the book before it went into print, it stays for the world to know.

My father is a multi-talented personality. Although I didn't inherit any of his talents, I have had a complete share of his love.

My coach, Karl-Heinz, has been the source of many successful ideas and strategic inputs that have taken my career on a constant and consistent rise to success. He is a living genius and I am grateful for his dedication and commitment towards my success, as a professional and as a person.

My publisher and editor, Sohin, puts me in debt with his kindness and his tolerance. He is an amazing soul.

Priyanka is my lifeline. When I am travelling, my company rides on her shoulders. She practically lives my life in my absence. She is the light that brightens up everyone's day at work, I know she does mine.

Mahavir, Sudhir, Asha and Tarsi, my extended team, ensure that goodness flows my way, for when trouble arises, they solve it before it gets to me. They all do a smashing job of keeping me on top of the world.

Coco, my little Yorkshire Terrier, is my indulgence. She is a bundle of pure love. She has a broken leg, but there is nothing broken in her spirit.

Special thanks to Reshma, Cyrus and Dolly, who helped make the book a seamless read, saving you the constant squints of trying to make sense of grammatical errors.

My readers humble me. Your curiosity about my world makes me responsible for creating one that you will grow bigger in. Thank you for being a part of my purpose and my journey.

CONTENTS

A PRAYER

Dubai International Airport is a shopper's paradise. Standing in the middle of the desert, its largest selling product is sand. Every second shop has on display, an array of sand art souvenirs. The number one thing to do here is 'spend money'. Spread over 8,500 acres, housing multiple stores and boutiques, it seems like a conspiracy to empty your pockets before you fly home. From sand to cars to diamonds to real estate, there is something here to tempt everybody.

It didn't seem like 3.50 am. The entire airport was lit up and buzzing with people. Transactions rolled incessantly in the duty free stores. Aircraft were landing, and aircraft were taking off. People were moving in and out of the country at the rate of 300-odd people per minute.

"Excuse me," Sarah almost knocked over the coffee from the man's tray with her elbow. He caught the mug before it toppled off and stared at her, alarmed, cursing under his breath.

"I'm sorry," she apologized with a momentary turn of her head and then darted off in the direction of Zone B, which the signboard indicated was a seven-minute walk.

"Damn it. Damn it," she cursed as she stopped to kick the black stilettos off her feet. Clutching them in her hands, she made a run for Gate 62.

"This is the last and final call for Ms. Sarah Jones travelling to New York on Flight SL502. You are requested to get to Gate 62 wherever you are. Please note, this is the last and final call," a man with a Middle Eastern accent announced, his voice blaring through the terminal loud and clear. Everyone in her way could tell that she was Sarah Jones and was heading for Gate 62.

Sarah had come in three hours early to the airport only to find out, in the end, that she was about to miss her flight. She had spent her time shopping without keeping a tab of the time flying by, until she heard her name announced. The purpose of being at the airport was to take a flight, but the temptation to possess 'things' became bigger. Sometimes we go adrift from our agendas, something that Sarah had frequently been doing in life. We are here for a reason, but we land up pursuing something else, and end up having something completely different, which we never intended to start with.

Some people miss their flight because they are late while some others miss it even though they reach early. When the mind is cluttered and spinning with confusion, time, opportunities and luck become secondary. A clear mind *creates* time; it *creates* opportunities and is a magnet for good luck.

"I'm coming. Damn it!" Sarah muttered out loud desperately.

Gate 54 was visible now, and there were no more announcements. Sarah's face was turning pale with all the running. The black hood of her Bebe sweatshirt was flying behind her, giving a surreal bounce to her curly blond hair. She was less than a minute from reaching her gate. Her phone rang in the back pocket of her denim jeans. She pulled it out, not slowing her pace. The name Mike flashed on the screen as she looked at her phone, not taking her eyes off her destination.

"Not now," she muttered. She could not take the call right now. Sarah had not told Mike that she had rescheduled her flight to arrive a day earlier. Her plan was to 'surprise' him and to know for sure whether he was cheating on her. Either she would catch him red-handed with another woman or she would settle to marry him. She needed to know for sure. This was her way of deciding her destiny.

Sarah and Mike had been dating on and off for over a year. Mike was dreamy and Mike was hot. As much as they had their differences, mainly over infidelity, whenever Mike came back apologizing, Sarah would forgive him. Mike had a sincere side in him which invariably melted Sarah's heart. How Sarah wished that side of him would last. And then he had those irresistible, dreamy eyes and his baby smile. *How could someone that good-looking be capable of malicious intent?* This was her foolish rationale. Sarah and Mike would get back together until she would walk out on him again, on suspicion or partial evidence of dishonesty.

Sarah was in a relationship that was slowly destroying her sanity, her happiness and her peace. In the name of love, what she was feeling in her heart was pain and restlessness. She knew Mike's ways, and she knew his weaknesses. She knew his interest in women other than her. What more did she want to know? Would he change his ways? Was she important enough for him to initiate that change? That question was as foolish as the answer it would fetch. No one changes for anyone. We change in accordance to our thinking, to our principles and to our postulates. You can inspire change in another, but you can't be the cause of it.

Why be with one person when your heart slips for another? Why commit to someone, when what you want is to be free to wear your heart on your sleeve? Why the duality where you want to be loved and then risk it for the meaningless indulgence of a few minutes of pleasure? That seems more like the definition of being *lost* rather than being in *love*.

Sarah's misunderstanding of what she really wanted had put her in the eye of a storm, for that is the fate of the person who is a muse for the non-committal lover.

After window-shopping most of the branded stores in the airport, Sarah had stopped at Ralph Lauren to buy a shirt for Mike. The moment she saw it on the mannequin, she felt like it was made for him. The shirt was a pink and blue chequered print and she knew that he would look stunning in it. And that was the exact reason she changed her mind at the cash-counter—'he would look stunning in it'! That's not how she wanted him to project himself to other women.

The sign to Gate 62 glowed up ahead. Gate 62 was deserted. Unlike the long, winding queues at the other gates she passed, this one was empty.

"Hey wait. Please," she begged as she almost hauled herself at the airline staff behind the counter. The overly large man got up and adjusted his 'thwab', a long white ankle-length robe that the Middle Eastern men wear. He tapped his badge and looked at Sarah, holding his breath. It would be a tough one to offload a lady as pretty as her.

"Ms. Sarah Jones?" Ali raised his thick brow, concerned.

"Yes," she barely whispered, panting heavily. The gloss on her lips made them look delicious. The mascara in her eyes gave her a real 'damsel in distress' look. A loose strand of blonde hair was dangling across her cheek, flying to and fro with her breath. Sarah was exceedingly pretty.

"Sorry Ma'am. The flight is closed. We are offloading your bags now," he said nervously in his Arabic accent, barely keeping his eyes off her cleavage, which was visible through the two buttons that had popped off Sarah's sweatshirt from all the running.

"No. You can't do that," she panted. "I have to get on the flight. Please. I will lose my job. I will lose everything. I must get on that flight," she lied, grabbing the counter lest she faint with all the stress. Getting home to Mike was frightful enough and now missing the flight would leave her future hanging in doubt—'is he the right one, or is he not?'

The man stared at her breasts for a few seconds, totally oblivious to her plea and then got on his walkie-talkie and spoke something in Arabic, not taking his eyes off her.

She looks so pretty and pretty women don't deserve to be miserable, he thought.

Sarah grabbed his arm as the man continued to growl into his walkie. The touch of a white lady was building up the intensity in his voice. He was finding it difficult to breathe with the electric energy that was shooting up his arm and stinging his brain. His eyes were battling between her cleavage, her hand on his arm and the aircraft that stood majestically behind the large windows, ready to take flight to the skies.

The walkie went silent, and Sarah's head reeled. She waited with bated breath for the verdict as Ali stared lustfully at her. The walkie crackled again and Ali yelled some more Arabic into it. He wanted to get her on the flight and be her hero.

"God. Get me on this flight. That's all I will ever ask, ever," Sarah prayed hard, squeezing Ali's arm as she did. The walkie blared and crackled in response. All she could hear was a few people yelling in the background.

"Come with me," Ali jerked her hand off his arm as they both sprinted off onto the aerobridge as an answer to her prayer.

With her shoes in her hand and her hair bobbing into her hoodie, Sarah ran as fast as she could to keep up with Ali.

A flight attendant stood at the mouth of the aircraft with one hand on the door. She stretched out the other hand, dramatizing the urgency for her to speed up. Sarah ran the fastest she ever had. Ali was in step with her. She held out her boarding pass at the totally startled ground staff, who grabbed it, ripped off one part and thrust the other into her hand. Sarah stepped into the aircraft and turned around to face Ali, who had stopped at the entrance.

"Thank you," she panted, folding her hands along with her shoes.

"You are beautiful," he smiled, his Arabic accent making the compliment exotic.

"Thank you, God," Sarah walked shakily through the aisle looking for her seat, 26D.

⋯⋯⋯⋯⋯⋯⋯

THE TAKEOFF

⋯⋯⋯⋯⋯⋯

"I'd like a Glenfiddich please, neat," Paul ordered his drink and Glenda, the flight attendant, smiled sensuously at him.

Paul was a billionaire, best known for his good looks and his indulgence in luxury yachts. He was featured in numerous business magazines, sometimes even making it to the cover. The women often debated whether his dreamy face attracted more attention than his money. His dimples, his perfectly set teeth, his athletic body, his maturity, and his sensitivity made him one of the most eligible bachelors in New York.

Glenda knew who Paul was, and was delighted with the opportunity to be at his service. Meeting rich men, getting invited to their parties and asking favours from them were some of the reasons that Glenda had taken up a job with the airline. She had worked hard to get promoted to the first class section.

Paul smiled, turning his gaze towards the window. He ran his hand through his long salt-and-pepper hair and let a finger idly twirl on one lock.

"Coming up, Mr. Thomas," Glenda giggled playfully, tossing her hair over her shoulder flirtatiously as she turned and walked down the aisle.

It had been a long day for Paul. His flight back marked the signing of a six-hundred-million-dollar deal that he had struck for his new energy plant in Chicago. He was powerful, he was handsome and he was mysterious. Paul looked around the first class cabin as he removed his Armani jacket and placed it on the hook for Glenda to stow away for him. The first class had only one more passenger—an old man who occupied a seat across the other end of the aisle. His eyes were closed and he seemed to be meditating, sitting up alert with a soft expression of calm on his face. Paul stared hard as though trying to place him, but he didn't look familiar. He would have the entire section pretty much to himself. Paul smiled at the thought.

Success means different things to different people. Those who have it, think they can buy the world with their power, people included. Those who don't have it, think they can scrape it off those who do. There are those who don't care about the result of what they do and are disconnected from success. And then there are a select few, who don't care about what they get, as long as they love what they do.

Success had lost its charm for Paul. He was successful. The question that haunted him was 'what now?' What lies after one has achieved everything? What purpose did his life and work hold after all purposes were fulfilled? Success meant nothing to Paul. He had had enough of it.

Paul quickly downloaded the emails on his iPad. It was going to be a long fifteen hours to New York and he was hoping to get some work done during that time. With the way Glenda was sashaying around him taking his coat away, he had his doubts if he would get a chance to have his space. Women were attracted to Paul like moths were to light. Besides his good looks and his money, there was also the fact that he was a thorough gentleman. His single status was acknowledged by the flirtatious behaviour of the ladies who first looked at his hand for the missing wedding band, and then lustfully at his face.

Paul was one of those people whose life seemed to be straight out of a Hollywood film with all the fame, power and fancy lifestyle. But life had taken an unexpected turn. The wealthier he got, the sadder he felt. The more things he acquired, the emptier he felt. Giving money away to charity didn't give him the fulfilment he sought. Withdrawing from his manic social lifestyle didn't bring him the sanity he needed. He felt as though something was missing in this equation of life—something big, something significant, something that was bigger and beyond the success that he had built. He didn't know what he was looking for, and so he didn't know how to find it.

One of the flight attendants had started with the takeoff announcements and safety instructions. A video on the features of the aircraft and the escape routes in case of emergency played on every screen, somehow reassuring the passengers that every eventuality was planned for.

"He is Paul Thomas, the billionaire," Glenda whispered to her envious colleague. "And he is a charmer," she winked with the anticipated delight of spending the next fifteen hours serving a man whose total net-worth could buy off the airline she worked for. Or maybe that was her exaggerated imagination. She wanted to feel good about being in his powerful company. She was going to fuss over him the entire journey and was hoping he would reciprocate. If it hadn't been for the one other occupied seat in first class, the section would have been sealed off for his indulgence, from the rest of the aircraft and the rest of the world.

*****

"I think you are in my seat," Sarah said politely to the young man who kept staring at her, totally oblivious to his intrusion on her seat. It took Jim a few seconds to realize that she was talking to him, and another few seconds to digest what she was saying.

Jim had to move his gadget collection, which he had spread out on Sarah's seat for the journey. He first dropped his iPad on the floor, then clumsily wrapped the wires of his overly large headphones, snatched his iPhone and all his various gadget cases, as Sarah waited patiently for her seat. There was a television screen in front with the latest movies queued up and the young fellow had his own arrangement for the flight. Sarah shook her head, amused by his over-indulgence with technology.

Sarah settled down in her seat much to the delight of Jim, a young teenager. Jim had been happy to have the seat next to him empty, in the hope of stretching and having some additional space. He was already too tall for the seat and was not too happy about being trapped in the little space. One look at Sarah and his emotions went from disappointment to delight. Having a hot, young woman as a co-passenger for the entire duration of the flight was taking his conversation with the boys back home to a whole new level of discussion.

"I believe this is your book," said Sarah, plucking out a book from the seat pocket in front of her. She glanced at the cover, 'Have You Lived Before This Life?' by L. Ron Hubbard. Sarah was quite surprised that a young man like him was interested in the afterlife, or for that matter, in past lives.

Sarah turned to take a good look at Jim as he extended his hand to take his book. He was a teenager, but his eyes had a depth that Sarah couldn't decipher in that brief glance.

"You believe in past lives?" Sarah smiled.
Jim chuckled. He shook his head. He was quite taken aback by

the question and wasn't prepared with an answer. "Well," he said and then paused a few seconds as Sarah settled into her seat. She turned to Jim waiting for the answer.

"Well," he muttered again. "I don't believe in past lives. It would be silly to say I believe that. I *know* I have lived before, I don't believe I have lived before. I *know* it, as have you," Jim saw the blank look on Sarah's face and muttered, "maybe."

"This is going to be an interesting flight," Sarah let out a long sigh and smiled at Jim. "Can I see this book?"

Jim nodded in approval.

Jim was seventeen and he was unkempt. He was tall and lean. His blond hair was trimmed back neatly and the freckles on his face added to the texture. He was particularly excited about the tan that he had managed to pull off on his short holiday, sunbathing in Dubai. Dressed in a white hooded full sleeve T-shirt and unwashed blue jeans, he looked like a typical American teenager.

Jim was a self-contained unit, a young man who was perfectly happy in his own company. He carried his world wherever he went. His mother often said that he was too wise for his age. She worried about him when he took off for his occasional reclusive bouts. Jim was a thinker. He had more questions than the world held answers for him. He looked deep at life. He probed the intention rather than the actions, a trait not common to youngsters his age. He was the confidante of many, but kept his worries and his aspirations to himself.

Although he normally wore a solemn expression, Jim's face was lit up with excitement, something he had not felt in a while. He kept bumping the passenger ahead, who was swearing every time Jim's knee jerked into his seat. Jim had come to Dubai with his parents for a holiday, but had to cut his trip short because his soccer practice had started a week earlier than scheduled. Jim was passionate about soccer. Returning earlier also had an added incentive of having the entire house to himself for a full week. That in his world spelt 'freedom'. Solitude was Jim's favourite indulgence. He enjoyed his own company. His books, his gadgets and his ever-alive mind kept him busy, curious and happy.

Sarah's phone beeped as she settled in her seat and wore her seat belt.

"Are you okay, baby? I love you." Mike had sent her a message. *This was so unlike Mike. He is definitely cheating on me.* Sarah squirmed with the thought. Why else would he send her such a message? Sarah could not remember the last time that Mike sent her a lovey-dovey message on his own initiative. He messaged when she messaged. How come the sudden expression of affinity? Sarah couldn't make peace with the message. She was in a state of turmoil and would question anything at the moment, even an act of love.

Mental chaos taints one's perception—one sees through the filter of that turmoil, one derives comprehension through that mental mess; therefore all one creates in that state of negativity is a further extended muddle. One's state of mind becomes evident in one's immediate world. The state of one's world thus becomes an evidence of one's state of mind.

Sarah wanted to call Mike, but then she didn't want him to know she was flying out. Men show extra love when they are guilty. Sarah knew that. She was a writer, and she was a lover who had been hurt often enough, but had not learnt well. She would call him when she landed and would tell him she was taking off. If he were actually cheating on her, Mike would take the bait of his last night out before his commitment to her began its umpteenth round.

Sarah put her phone away and looked at Jim, who stared ahead at the blank TV screen without blinking. Jim had got Sarah's attention. No one had spoken to her about past lives before. She was unsure about her whereabouts other than this life and she wasn't sure if she was going to get another chance again. How did Jim get the idea, or know about past lives as he said he did? Had she lived before? Would she live again? She wanted to have a chat with him.

My parents are away for a week. I have the house to myself. I am a soccer champion. I have a pretty lady next to me and it's a long journey. Jim was busy deciphering the connection of all these events. He hadn't felt this lucky in a long time.

It was not Sarah's physical beauty that had him awestruck, though she did look lovely. Being a soccer star, he was used to getting attention from the girls, but, unlike a soccer star, he didn't reciprocate the attention. But there was something else about Sarah; it was her presence, it was her vibe that had struck a chord with him. Sarah's energy seemed to have depth, meaning and a pain that he could connect and relate with.

The plane was moving out of the parking bay now. The man on the aisle seat adjacent to Sarah's let out a loud sigh. He was Indian; his dark skin and the three ash drawn lines on his forehead suggested he was from the southern part of India. He wore an off-white embroidered silk kurta, which was totally out of contrast with his dark blue jeans. His hair was parted on one side and sat still with a coating of oil. His eyes were swollen from lack of sleep and his lips quivered with a *mantra* that he was chanting softly to himself. He brought his hands close to his chest, closed his eyes and then mumbled a prayer as the plane taxied towards the runway.

Sarah was intrigued by Indians. They were mystical; they were wise and they had culture, something she missed in her own country. Sarah decided to chat with him later. Maybe he could give her an interesting storyline for her next article.

Sarah leaned forward to look out of the window. Jim had sunk further back into his seat to give her a better view. This was it. She had taken a major step towards discovering a truth that she had refused to confront. She held the armrest tight with a strange nervousness. Sarah was counting on divine intervention to give her the strength to face up to the truth, so that she could map the course of her life, with or without Mike.

It's funny how people look for signs outside even when their heart is signalling them the way all the time. There are no signboards in life; your inner voice and your inner knowledge are enough to lead you in the direction of your highest evolution.

*****

"What's with Captain Robert today?" Glenda nudged Cathy, her confidante and partner-in-crime on long haul flights.

"What's with *you* today?" Cathy tried to brush off an indulgence in a meaningless conversation about men that Glenda was so fond of.

"He seems a bit uptight today," Glenda continued despite Cathy's disinterest in her intuitive abilities.

"I have a feeling he will put in his papers soon. He seems a

little off the job. Remind me next time not to get on his flight."
Glenda shook her head.

"He has this weird look. Seems like he has lost weight too, not
in a good way though." Glenda continued with her blabber and
Cathy only pretended to listen.

With the cabin lights dimmed, the passengers were settling
in to get ready for the fifteen-hour flight. Some had already
pushed their seats back once the flight attendants had taken
their positions for takeoff. Some were cuddled up uncomfortably
in their seats, drifting in and out of the state of helpless
sleepiness. A few brave ones were reading the newspaper at
the ungodly hour, and yet a few had found a movie that would
engage them till breakfast was served. And then there were
a select few who were awake—alert, and intuitive to a vibe
that seemed out of the ordinary, a vibe that nudged them to
edginess that something was wrong ... terribly wrong.

The captain made takeoff announcements as the aircraft
taxied to its turn on the runway. A large FedEx Carrier took its
position ahead giving SL502 three minutes to take off from the
ground and penetrate into the dawn of a new day.

✶✶✶✶✶

Sarah shifted uncomfortably in her seat. She was not supposed
to be on this flight. This was a flight that she would not forget.
She had never gone snooping on a guy before. But it was
important for her to know. Mike was 'the one' or so she
thought. If she was wrong about Mike this time, she would
bury her suspicions forever. Maybe he had changed. She so
badly hoped he had changed.

Muttuswamy kept glancing left and right to catch the view

outside from the windows on either side. Sarah turned to him and smiled as he peeped in her direction, but he quickly looked the other way. He kept mumbling to himself and counting some numbers on his fingers. The nervousness on his face kept growing. He wiped off some sweat from his forehead, spreading the ash and merging the three lines into a smear.

Muttuswamy needed to clear his head. There was too much going on in his world. He snapped open his laptop. The seat belt sign was on and the instructions for electronic devices to be switched off were already given. The aircraft was three minutes away from takeoff and yet Muttuswamy violated all aviation rules and furiously began to write on his blog. This couldn't wait. He had to write. He was compelled to write, as though not out of his own volition. Writing was something he often did to get more distance and clarity on the thoughts that were floating aimlessly in his mind, consuming his space, his energy and his sanity. Although Muttuswamy wrote to find answers for himself, when he shared his thoughts through his blog, his followers consumed every word he expressed, for they resonated with their own higher state of mind. His words dissolved their confusion and delivered clarity as they did for him.

Life is a topic that is a mystery to most. Why am I here? What is my purpose? Why do I behave the way I do, even though I don't stand for that behaviour? How do I make a change when I can't even locate the source of the problem that is keeping me down?

If destiny is all-primary, then was I born a victim to my future? Are we all victims of destiny? Or do we have the power to create our own future and define destiny as we do so?

Life is a mystery to most.

Some of us, however, are on the path to unravel the missing link in this puzzle that keeps us small—that keeps us believing in a power source that is external to us. If power, faith, greatness, and knowing are external, then we are at the mercy of that source to grant us our share. There are a few, though, who are driven to bring down the curtain of falsities which keeps us tied to mortality, which keeps our beliefs and vision limited to a fear of the unknown, which keeps us pinned to a mass mentality—that you are a nobody in this vast universe.

You are somebody. I sure feel like one—a someone that has forgotten to be me.

The universe seems vast perhaps because I have made myself small.

Does our time on Earth define the length of our existence? Or do we have an existence beyond the end of our time here?

Where am I headed? That question goes a bit deeper, a bit beyond this life. And if I could define the next destination, would I continue to be as I am today and continue to do what I am doing?

My five-year-old granddaughter asked me some innocently-put yet thought-provoking questions, 'Grandpa when are you going to die? Where will you go once you are dead? What will you do then?'

I still do not have an answer to these questions, although I have an inkling.

How can I think of the journey ahead when I am sunk so deep in trudging painfully on this path called 'life'?

It is the man at the end of his life who is closer to the truth. But his answers are still vague and unclear when he is asked to sum up his term.

What was the point of my life?
Did I discover who I really am as a result of my living?
Did I do as I say and did I feel what I really wanted to?

I have seen people hours before their end. Did they look peaceful? Did they feel special? Did they look closer to their salvation? They were far from it.

How did life serve them in bringing to fore the answer to the questions that had evaded them the most: 'Who am I? Why am I here?'
We were born into amnesia. Are we going to die into another abyss of mysteries? Or will the end set us free?

My profession binds me—I cannot 'see' my future as I see it for others—but I feel that the end is near. I feel that a new beginning waits on the other side of the material end.

My granddaughter's questions are still guiding me forward. 'What am I going to do when it all ends?' In predicting the future for others, I had missed creating one for myself—a future beyond the material mortality, a future where I would head when it all appears to end.

Muttu's fingers paused as he looked at the one-bar signal on his laptop. Syncing the Internet from his phone to his laptop was going to cost him a lot of money, but this message was important. He rubbed his ash-smudged forehead with the back of his hand and then hit POST making his blog go live for his 1.6 million hungry followers, seconds before takeoff.

*****

Jim had settled into watching a movie. He was watching *The Matrix* for the umpteenth time to the point where he knew the scenes and dialogues by heart. The movie was real to him. He saw reality in the science-fiction that rolled out on the screen. With the large headphones on his head, he had cut himself off from the rest of the world. Once every two minutes, he would glance at Sarah and draw an inch closer, feel her warmth and settle back into his world. Although she was much older to him, Jim felt inexplicably drawn to her like a moth is to fire.

Paul had gulped his Glenfiddich and was waiting for the buzz to set in. Strangely, he felt alert—as if his brains were fighting the temporary bout of euphoria from the whisky. He would get himself another shot once the flight took off. It was late and he had had a long day. By now the alcohol would have normally started the countdown of drowsiness but Paul felt unusually awake. Maybe it was the victory of his business deal. Maybe it was his disconnect from that victory. He felt it, but he didn't feel it—a state that made him wonder what was wrong with him. He tried to be happy about his achievements, but didn't. What he felt was a different feeling, a disturbing feeling. The anxiety that he felt in his stomach was pulling his attention. *What could possibly go wrong?* He looked out of the window and then sighed back into his chair.

"I hope they all sleep easy," the flight attendants prayed to the gods of the skies so that they could have a restful flight.

*****

The FedEx Carrier sped on the runway and then lunged into the sky, blinking like a spacecraft as it merged into the darkness.

"Darn," Captain Robert muttered as the Air Traffic Control asked Flight SL502 to wait in line for two more arrivals on the runway. That would push the takeoff further by another six minutes.

Captain Robert was in his late forties but looked much older. The frown lines on his forehead dug deep. The lines around his eyes fanned out from his brow to his cheeks. His face looked weathered. His eyes held in them depths of sadness. He had lost a lot of weight recently and his uniform hung loosely on him.

Robert had been toying with the idea of suicide for weeks now. Life had lost meaning for him. He wanted to die and end his misery. It was only last night that he had settled in with the plan to end his life, yet again. However, like most anxious and psychotic people do, he reported for work when he was called in an emergency to fill in for this flight.

Robert had a new plan—to die while at work, mid-air at thirty-five thousand feet above sea level.

First Officer Tom was restless, brushing his hair obsessively. He was in his early thirties and was a charming young man. He looked like a fine blend between Brad Pitt and Ben Stiller, his mood defining the look. Most of the flight attendants had a crush on him and gave him the attention that he welcomed. He ensured he worked out every day to keep his sexual appeal high.

Tom was in a committed relationship. His girlfriend called him a thinker, a philosopher and often commented that he was in the wrong job. With the words of wisdom that sometimes would find a way in his daily talks, she was convinced he would have made an excellent spiritual leader. Tom however found his peace in the skies. Being away from the ground and closer to the rest of the universe brought him an elation that pulled him through his time on the ground. Tom was more than happy to fill in when the other captains couldn't report for duty. When he was roaming the skies, he felt free.

Although Tom had been flying for five years, recently his girlfriend Nina had been having nightmares about his flying. The nightmares were getting more frequent and she had been insisting that Tom should take a break for a few months, or just some time off. The nightmares were taking a toll on Nina, and Tom was planning to take two weeks off so she could calm down. He loved Nina, but he could not explain to her his urge to fly. It was as though it gave him wings. It was as though it was a route to his freedom. Freedom from what? He couldn't tell. But he felt the trap the minute he landed on ground. Since he couldn't explain this feeling, he kept it to himself. He would take Nina on a holiday and hope that her worries would be put to rest.

Captain Joe was seated in the flight crew resting cabin. He would relieve Captain Robert a few hours into the flight, and then the first officer and he would rotate, taking turns. It was a long flight and they were good at swapping responsibilities.

Everything was in order. Everything and everyone was functioning as planned. You do this and this and this and you will land safely fifteen hours later at your destination. But little does one know that despite doing this, and this, and this— the actions that guarantee a certain set of consequences—the desired and the predicted consequence can be altered by the thought and counter intention of just one person present in the game. As much as the process is critical for success, so is the intention of every person involved.

Robert glared at the flight that swooped in for landing. He placed his hand on his chest pocket. A little plastic pouch holding two capsules sat close to his heart. Each had enough powder in them to paralyze a hundred-pound beast within minutes, leading to its certain death. The label however said 'Vitamin C'. He tapped his knee; the turmoil was penetrating through his body. *Don't do it!* The voice rang through his head. Robert fidgeted in his seat, his eyes fixating on the next aircraft.

"You okay, Captain?" Tom picked up on his edginess. Robert stared on ahead, silent.

What did he expect Robert to say? *'No, I'm not okay! I am going to commit suicide in a few hours!'* Tom knew Robert was not okay but hoped to hear a comforting and reassuring answer so he could shut up his inner knowing and renounce the responsibility of altering the consequence that Robert's insanity would bring.

When someone has the control of the vehicle you are aboard, his problem is your problem. When someone is a part of your journey in life, his problem is your problem. When someone has a stake in your success, his problem is your problem. Confront it. Resolve it.

Robert turned his face to the right, his eyes following the aircraft that had just landed. He placed his hands hastily on the control. The second the voice from the control room crackled on the radio, he propelled the engines into motion without waiting to hear out the instructions. Tom was a little taken aback, but then ignored Robert's hastiness. The sky was clear on the left. No landing aircraft were in sight, so Tom was at ease.

The aircraft inched into takeoff position and the red lights on the runway shone bright as though sending a warning signal to those who had tuned themselves into the future. And with the job done, they turned green.

Robert pushed the buttons aggressively. His face was expressionless, as though holding a pit of dark secrets, secrets that were brewing up a new destiny for the day that lay ahead. Tom crossed his heart and kissed his hand in prayer. Robert pushed the throttle a few inches and that set the aircraft growling and racing over the concrete as the three hundred people aboard braced themselves for takeoff. The aircraft caught speed and then, as he pushed the throttle back further, the aircraft lunged off its wheels and tore the wind, heading for its destiny thirty-five thousand feet up into the sky.

DECISIONS MAKE DESTINY

Ten minutes into the flight, a buzzer went off to release the flight attendants from their position; Cathy popped her cheerful head inside the cockpit.

"Coffee, Captains?"

"Yes, two black coffees please," First Officer Tom ordered for both of them. "It's a long flight," he nodded towards Robert.

"Aye aye. Sir. Two hot coffees coming up," Cathy chirped, nodding her head; her fake hair stayed set, showing no motion. The mood in the service galley was bright. Tom seemed to have worked his charm on the crew.

Robert pulled out the little plastic bag from his chest pocket. Tom eyed him unsuspectingly.

"Vitamins? Man!" First Officer Tom sniggered. He wanted to make a joke but refrained from doing so. Robert seemed to be in a foul mood and Tom decided to stay out of his way. When they landed, over a drink, he would bring up the topic of Robert's health and his reclusive attitude. Every captain had to go through regular medical exams at set intervals, but Tom was concerned that Robert had lost a lot of weight lately and looked preoccupied all the time.

Robert clenched his fists. He was losing control. He was losing his mind. He had to stay in control. His breathing was rapid and he was trying hard to fight the nausea that was building up. His head felt like it would split into two. He should have stayed home and stuck to his plan. Getting on the flight now seemed like a really bad idea.

Robert knew that something was terribly wrong with him; he wanted to live and be happy, but this growing urge to end his life had been driving him insane. He knew that he was sinking into a pit of negativity and self-destruction. But knowing that gave him no control over the streaks of insanity that were erupting in the daily handling of his life.

Every person whose behaviour violates his own moral code knows that something is wrong. He knows that this is not his inherent nature. He knows that a compulsion beyond his control is driving his thoughts and his actions. He knows that he is a victim of that compulsion and all he can do is witness his own downfall, slowly but steadily, in a state of utter helplessness. In addition, such is his luckless fate that the more he tries to make things right, the more wrong he commits. Robert was caught in that trap of insanity.

He turned to Tom, who was staring ahead at the sky, clueless about the strange phenomenon that was building up within Robert.

Do it. This time just do it. The voice screamed in Robert's head again.

"You all right, Captain?" Tom smiled politely in a desperate attempt to get some reassurance. *Why couldn't he just say he was okay?* Tom shifted uncomfortably. Even a response like, *'No, I am not okay'* would have been acceptable. But Robert chose silence as his answer, leaving Tom in a flurry of worry.

Robert's pale face and his solemn expression coupled with his silence were making Tom exceedingly nervous. *What could possibly be wrong with him? His problem didn't seem to be stemming from a health issue. With the look on Robert's face, he seemed to be in some emotional turmoil,* Tom thought.

Over the past few months, people around him had noticed that Robert had become impatient and aloof. Whether he was sad or angry, they could no longer tell. What they didn't know was that Robert was suffering mentally.

Flashes of Iraq would find their way into his thoughts at frequent intervals. The firing, the bombing, the dead bodies—they all crept into vision and blurred his reality. The commands, 'fire', 'kill', 'strike the enemy', echoed in his ears. He would feel a sudden, inexplicable impulse to kill and would land up hurting himself in his day-to-day life instead. Once, he had cut his hand on a blade of a knife as he clenched it in his hand in a moment of anxiety. Another day, he had the impulse to beat the life out of a chauffeur who spoke too loudly in the car.

Robert had quit the U.S. Air Force and stepped down from his position of Major so that he could sleep in peace. He didn't want to kill anymore. He didn't want to load up the fighter and go on an air-hunt, gunning people down or blowing them up. It had made him feel like an alien, almost non-human, for how could one human being kill another for no logical reason? The people that died in the name of war had nothing to do with the war in the first place. They were not even the enemy. The enemy stayed alive while the innocent died. However, the command implanted in the officer was to kill, so that the keepers of war could play their game of insanity.

Coming back to civilian life was tougher than being in the army. Finding a resolve to problems and creating solutions was the kind of thinking he was not used to, for he was trained to destroy an obstacle. The way to solve a problem was to destroy it, kill it, or blow it up. He was a misfit. He had felt that he would have a better life outside the air force, but he couldn't stand the happiness, the sanity, and everything that defined a happy life. His hands compulsively itched to hold a gun, his nose longed to smell the ammunition, and his eyes yearned to see the sight of blood.

Training and serving in the armed forces takes a toll on a person's innate nature of compassion, rationality and sanity. Robert had paid the price during the term of his service. What he didn't know then was that he would continue to pay that price ... for the rest of his life.

Robert's wife and his two daughters had been his distraction from the madness that inhabited his mind. So he kept himself busy with his work and his family, for idleness would activate the commands that nudged the monster he was trying so hard to suppress. Now that they were gone, killed in a car accident, his mind had found an excuse to unleash the demon.

Robert's mind was made up. His uniform from the air force and his badges of glory were packed in his suitcase. He would put an end to the devil in his mind before it used him to hurt others. He would do the rounds with Captain Joe in a couple of hours. He would retire in the crew rest cabin and, there, he would consume the poison and die at thirty-five thousand feet in the sky—a destiny that would have added glory to his life during his term in the air force.

*****

Robert held one capsule in his hand as Cathy knocked and entered.

"Coffee for the Captains," she smiled, eyeing them both. They both seemed preoccupied.

"Coffee isn't good for health," Tom grinned at Cathy.

Robert turned the capsule and made a fist as he adjusted some knobs. *Don't do it. Do it now. Die. Kill.* Multiple voices conflicted in his head.

"Coffee makes the skin look old. Vitamin C however makes it youthful," Tom winked at Cathy and she smiled nervously.

Robert's breathing was now heavy as was his head.

Sensing the tension build up in the cockpit, Cathy made a quick exit. She would tell First Officer Tom to go easy on his small talk. Robert was not the same friendly person he used to be.

"First Officer," Robert looked at Tom sternly. "Vitamin C *is* good for the skin. It also protects you from cancer, which you lost your mother to." He popped open the capsule and stirred it into his cup.

Tom's mouth fell open with the spiteful comment that Robert had just made about his mother. *What the hell was wrong with him?* Tom's eyebrows crinkled with discomfort. He wouldn't fly with him again, he swore.

"Hey, no offence, Captain. I was just kidding," Tom apologized, fiddling with the controls. He was the First Officer and protocol needed him to treat the captain with respect. He may have been out of line with the humour, but Robert certainly had some misplaced emotions that were finding their outlet in a very hurtful manner.

Robert waited with bated breath as the coffee swirled for a few seconds, blending in the deadly infusion of hemlock and aconite, a toxic mix potent enough to kill a cow, slowly but surely.

He had bought the poison from a local drug peddler. It took him weeks to convince the peddler that his intention was suicide, not murder. The two capsules cost him his limited edition Rolex that he exchanged for the lethal dose of hemlock and aconite. 100 mg of hemlock is enough to cause death, which comes in the form of paralysis, where the mind is still awake but the body doesn't respond and the respiratory system shuts down. Probably the most famous hemlock poisoning was that of the Greek philosopher Socrates, who was condemned to death for impiety in 399 BC. Adding aconite to the mixture would cause arrhythmic heart function, leading to suffocation and then death.

What does poison taste like? Robert had wondered. "Most poisons taste horrible," the peddler had smirked. "There are a lot of poisons available in the market—rat poison, bug spray and more—so why do people come to me? Because the ones on the shelf are unpalatable. Bug spray, when ingested, will kill you. But you can't drink it even if you wanted to. You need a poison that is edible. Your body has to accept it first to kill you. That's what you exchange your Rolex for—a poison that you can consume."

Was he sure? A flash of doubt pierced in his already muddled mind. *Once he consumed the coffee, even a single sip, then there was no turning back. Did he really want to end it all? Was today going to be the last day of his life? Would this be the last flight he would ever take?* Dying in the cockpit was the closest he would come to dying in service. A sweat began to build up on his forehead and upper lip.

He just had to drink his coffee, like he always had, and it would grant him his death wish. Robert had often toyed with the idea of suicide but never gone through with it. His only solace in handling his repulsion to life was this idea that he could put an end to it.

"You mixed Vitamin C in your coffee?" Tom asked, trying to initiate conversation.

Robert was too lost in the chaotic churning of his mind to answer his question. If he didn't have the courage to drink this coffee today, he would still have a chance with the next capsule in the next flight, or even better, at home.

Tom was trying to hide his feelings and was keeping a straight face. He knew that Robert had served the U.S Air Force for fifteen years and had stepped down as Major after he lost his childhood friend in a mid-air collision over Iraq. The word in the captains' circle was that he had coaxed his friend on the assignment despite his urge to withdraw, and had blamed himself for his death ever since.

After a two-year sabbatical, Robert's wife had insisted that he return to his passion—flying. He was welcomed by Skyline Airways and flew over the globe commercially for a living.

It was when his family died in a car crash that Robert began to show signs of irrationality. As his wife and two daughters were breathing their last, Robert was mid-air, transporting people from New York to Dubai. He found out about the tragedy only fifteen hours after their death and reached for their funeral another fifteen hours later.

Tom could put Robert's life into perspective and feel empathetic towards him. He understood his negativity and his bitterness.

He too had lost his wife and knew how difficult it was to make peace with an empty home. It makes you miserable to the point where you can't stand others being happy. He could understand Robert's pain and forgive his hurtful comments.

Robert stared ahead, emotionless. He had no intention of not having the coffee and overcoming this insanity, which had manifested into action. His heart was skipping beats. In the moments to follow, the fate of his life, the dread of an unknown future, all lay simmering in a mug of coffee and his intention to drink it.

The capsules had been close to his heart for weeks. He carried them everywhere he went but never had been able to build up enough courage to go through with his plan. That he wanted to die, he was sure of, but he wasn't sure about dying alone. He didn't want a lonely death. He was already lonely in life.

To have another person there with him when he died would be a solace. It would be better than dying by himself, only to be discovered weeks later, if discovered at all. Who would miss him? Who would look for him? Who would care that he was missing?

First Officer Tom and the three hundred passengers aboard were now chosen as the companions in his death.

*****

Tom released the seat belt sign and started his announcements informing the passengers that they were cruising at 35,000 feet and welcoming them to enjoy the ride. The skies were clear, darkest before it neared dawn. The stars had huddled up in front as though meaning to form a barrier to prevent the aircraft from going further. Retreat seemed to be the command in the air. An aircraft blinked past the horizon. Robert watched it till it disappeared.

With all controls on autopilot, Tom relaxed and pulled out his phone. He smiled, looking at the photos that his girlfriend had sent him. He was carrying a big surprise gift for her. He flicked lazily through her pictures, often enlarging them to get a good look at her eyes. She looked so picture-perfect.

Tom's hand groped for the cup by his side and then looked for the coffee placed on the tray between the two seats, between him and Captain Robert. Cathy had placed the tray further on Tom's side and he missed seeing the cup to the left meant for him. He assumed that Robert had already picked up his cup. He wrapped his hand around the coffee cup on the right— Robert's cup— the coffee cup with the deadly mix of hemlock and aconite. It was still warm.

Tom picked up the coffee mug and continued browsing through the pictures on his mobile phone. He had forgotten all about the episode with Robert. He relished the warmth of the cup on his hands, totally unaware of the powder that had converted every molecule of the caffeinated water into a lethal poison that would first paralyze him and then kill him slowly.

Tom raised the cup to his lips and took a large sip. The coffee tasted stronger than usual. It was exactly what he needed to keep him awake for the duration of the flight. He turned towards Robert and smiled, "Good coffee."

Robert was too lost in his despair to notice his destiny settling into Tom's fate, his intention finding effect on Tom's life—for his cup of coffee was now consuming Tom's life.

*****

Muttuswamy had been waiting for the seat belt sign to go off. He jumped off his seat and plucked out his laptop from the overhead bin. Luckily, the seats next to him were empty so he could look into the future without being intruded upon by a nosy co-passenger.

Muttuswamy flipped open his laptop and opened up an application he had created himself—'Future Forever'. It was an advanced numerology application which was a digital compilation of all his astrological calculations. He took out his boarding pass and punched in the number of his flight, the number of his seat, the date and the time of departure. Numbers floated on his laptop and then settled into one box. He took a deep breath and sank into his chair.

Ever since Muttuswamy had boarded the flight, he had been experiencing a restlessness which had only grown since takeoff. He was tuned into the future and was doing what most people do when they see something they don't like —go into denial, the rationale being that *if I turn away, maybe it will go away.* But no matter what sequence of numbers Muttu took up, the future stayed firm, unchanged.

"These can't be the right numbers," he muttered. "Maybe the software is acting up." He quit the application and restarted it.

Predicting the future is a valuable ability to have. However, it becomes a limiting ability if it shows you your end. How can a future ever end? It would be a very naïve soothsayer who could only see as far as your body existed. Does the person's future and journey forward terminate with the last beat of his heart? Does one have a future after the end of his life? It would take a mighty evolved soul to predict one's journey into the future, far and beyond the term of the body.

Muttu, as he was known back home, was far more evolved than he gave himself credit for. He made less of his abilities even when they shone bright in service of others. Company plays a critical role in the growth and evolution of a person. When people around you think small, you introvert on your own abilities and your own evolution. When people around you live small, you shrink your thinking and your vision to fit into their company.

Of late, Muttu had begun to question his actions and his life. He had begun to rise to a bigger truth. The truth that he could see far beyond the future that he dared to tell others. When people came to consult him about their lives, he could see where they had been before this life and he could see where they were headed after the current one. He could see beyond reality. Muttu could see the future, the one that extends into eternity. By that estimation, his future along with the future of everyone else was safe, for what else could be the consequence if immortality and eternity was your inheritance?

Muttu kept his hand on his chest. Maybe it was the acidity that was troubling him. He took a quick glance at the Asian vegetarian meal that the flight attendant had served him and then immediately covered it back.

He looked around for comfort. Sarah was scribbling into her notepad and Muttu decided to do something he had never done before—make small talk with a stranger at half-past four in the morning.

"Hello," he hesitatingly tried to get Sarah's attention.

Just when Sarah had started to get over her obsession with Mike and pen down her thoughts for her article, she was interrupted. She sighed and looked at Muttu with her eyebrows raised.

"Where are you from?" he asked nervously in his Indian accent. He wanted to ask the less invasive questions before he got her to tell him her birthdate.

"New York," Sarah smiled.

Jim was shifting in his chair. He had not yet gathered the courage to speak to Sarah and this middle-aged Indian man was stealing his thunder.

"I'm Muttu from India," Muttu faked a smile. "What do you do?" he queried in the hope of a return question.

"I'm a writer," Sarah now shifted her weight in his direction while Jim tapped his feet anxiously. He did not like another man hunting in his territory.

"Wow, that's wonderful. What do you write?"

"Well, I write columns for the *New York Times.* I interview people from all over the world. I was in Dubai to interview a Sheikh for my upcoming column. However, what I really want to do," Sarah paused as though letting Muttu in on a carefully guarded secret, "is to write books."

"Then why don't you?" Muttu posed the logical question.

Jim's ears were glued to the conversation. He had expected Sarah to be a model or an actress, but a writer! She somehow seemed even more attractive to him.

"Well, I have already written a book. I am just stuck at writing the ending. When I sent it to my editor, he said that I don't have the depth as far as human emotions are concerned. So I left it at that. It sits incomplete on my bookshelf. I don't have the confidence to bring it to an empowering end," Sarah's tone and her face dropped while expressing the last sentence. Sarah had told him the truth about the editor, but what she had not told him was the whole truth—that the editor was also an ex-boyfriend. Their relationship had been rocky while it lasted and had not ended on a good note. She suspected his criticism of her writing stemmed more out of jealousy and vengefulness than a genuine concern for improvement.

Two other passengers on the seats behind had perked up, tuning into the conversation while munching on their early morning meal. While some passengers had started snoring at the back and the front, their sounds had synchronized into a rhythm.

"To *want to be* an author is qualification enough to be one," Muttu reassured her. "And maybe it's time to change your editor." At that comment, both Muttu and Sarah smiled. Muttu had hit the bull's-eye with his advice.

"What do you do?" Sarah asked the question which Muttu had started the conversation for. He had lost track of his purpose and gotten involved in his chat with Sarah. He had not expected this kind of honesty from a stranger.

"I am a clairvoyant, an astrologer," said Muttu nervously, his face turning a shade of pink as he said that.

"Oh, you see the future," Sarah said excitedly, shutting her notebook and putting it away. Muttu smiled. He was used to this kind of response. He had always got this response in his thirty years of practice as an astrologer. People were always curious to know their future, though not all were ready to face it.

The future is a mysterious tense; it keeps people worked up in the present. Everyone is headed for the future; some have plans for it, while others are just drifting along where it takes them. Moreover, when it comes to someone who can see it, he is the new best friend that people want, especially if he can tell you what you want to hear.

What's to ask about the future really? Anyone can be an astrologer. Look at the person's thoughts, his mental make-up and what he does in his present and any ordinary person can predict with seventy percent accuracy the state of affairs of another person's future.

"What can you tell?" Sarah asked curiously.

"Anything. Any question really," Muttu shrugged. He bit his lip nervously. Did he really want to know the answer?

"Will I ever finish my book?" Sarah bit the tip of her finger. What she really wanted to ask was if she would marry Mike, if Mike was loyal to her. However, she didn't want to begin with a personal question. A book was more professional and even if he said that her career as an author wasn't meant to be, she wouldn't be as disappointed as she would be if he predicted that Mike wouldn't be the man in her future.

"What's your date of birth?" Muttu posed the real question and his heart stopped as Sarah hesitated.

Jim was listening with curiosity. He had estimated twenty-two. That would make her only five years elder and that was an age difference he was willing to ignore.

"Er, sixth of March, 1974."

Muttu opened his laptop with nervous fingers and Jim almost choked on his coke. She was fifteen years elder to him. *Darn the astrologer,* he cursed mentally for breaking his little bubble of infatuation. *But what the heck, Demi Moore married Ashton Kutcher who was about ten years younger than her,* so he was still in the game.

The date was the answer that Muttu was looking for, to look into her future and see where her life was headed. If a long life lay in wait for her, he could go to sleep peacefully knowing that the flight would land safely in fourteen hours at its destination. Their fate was, after all, intertwined ever since they had boarded the same flight.

Predicting the future had become very stressful for Muttu, especially when he was having visions of his own life while looking at the future of others. How does one continue with one's life knowing that his end is near, that the game will be up soon, knowing that the seer will soon lose his sight and his vision forever? Muttu had been preparing, had been discovering and trying to see beyond, into the future beyond his end. Was it close? Was he ready?

Muttu tapped at the keys furiously. Eight boxes held in them four numbers each. As Muttu pressed 'enter', all the numbers spun in a flurry and rested in one box that drained the blood off his face. This was exactly what he did not want to see. His mouth had turned dry and the image of the screen blurred in front of his eyes. Of all the predictions that he had made in his life, he had hoped that he was wrong about this one – for Sarah's destiny held the certainty of his.

"Where were you born?" Muttu's voice seemed stuck in his throat.

"New York," Sarah smiled nervously, sensing Muttu's dismay.

"What time?" Muttu continued despite the spell of uneasiness that had consumed his body.

"I don't know. I never bothered to find out," Sarah shrugged.

Muttu punched in some more numbers, but the numbers from that box did not budge. They all stayed there despite Muttu's desperate attempts at getting them to rearrange in the other seven empty boxes.

"So, am I meant to be an author?" Sarah leaned as far as she could near him through the aisle seat.

"You will finish your book. It is a masterpiece, I can see that." Muttu looked at Sarah, trying to conceal his worry.

Sarah would finish writing her book, that was clearly indicated by the one number, which was in the right box, and that left her with the next five hours to do so, for the end of five hours marked ... the end of her life.

*****

Paul had settled in and narrowed his options down to another shot of whisky and then to sleep the journey off. Glenda had plans of her own. She was alert and eager to be Paul's exclusive company for the rest of the flight. Cathy decided to take a nap as she didn't have a job to do. Glenda had taken over the one passenger in first class, for the old man at the other row was fast asleep.

"Some more whisky?" Glenda teased. A drunken man, at times, can be difficult but is always a very vulnerable man. She had learnt well on her job, flying wealthy businessmen to their destinations. Not every day was as exclusive as this, though.

"No, my dear," Paul said and surprised himself as he said that. "But bring me your most expensive jewellery in duty free." He looked at Glenda from the side of his eyes, his lips spreading into half a smile.

"Does it have to be one piece?" Glenda curled her lips seductively.

"No, but it has to be beautiful," Paul returned the flirtatious gesture.

"Oh," Glenda giggled, playing with her hair and then disappeared into the galley.

She caught Cathy's arm and gave her a full account of her mischief, quite against her will. She began to flip through the duty-free trolley and started to pick out all her favourite items on the tray. She would then leave it to the billionaire to choose which one he wanted to see on her.

Paul stretched his legs on the leg rest ahead. He reclined his chair and leaned back. He was getting ready for some entertainment.

Paul had been married for ten years and it had ended in a painful divorce. It was his most expensive indulgence, he often joked. He had been single for the last six years and stayed as far away from commitment as he could.

Although he boasted of a billion-dollar empire and often had the world's most gorgeous women by his side, what he seemed to enjoy more and more was his solitude. He liked being by himself. He didn't miss his ex-wife or his three children. It's not like he didn't care for or love them, but they, like him, were busy with their lives. What he would miss in the day was his time alone. Sitting in his room by his window, watching the starry sky and feeling the night-time breeze on his face brought him a serenity that he dared not speak about.

"This is a sign of old age taking over," his friend had said when he shared his feeling over a drink. That was the last time Paul ever let anyone know of his world of solitude.

It was not about old age. It was not about loneliness. Paul had so much of everything that he just wanted to be away from it all. It's the same feeling you get when you eat so much of what you like to eat that you don't like to eat it anymore. Just the sight of that food evokes a feeling of repulsion. The more he gave up, the better he felt. The more he gave away, the lighter he felt, as though a heavy burden was being lifted off him.

Paul was continuing his ways only to keep up with the image he had so strategically established. The women came and went for the world to see, but none made it to his bedroom. The cars rolled in and out, but none gave him the pride that he had once felt. The money zipped into his account faster than it ran out or could ever run out, but it didn't stir up his excitement as it used to. Paul's internal universe was taking a turn towards renunciation, whereas his social actions spoke otherwise.

"Shall I show you the trousseau?" Glenda giggled as she rolled in the duty-free trolley, with items opened in boxes for Paul to see. She wanted to see which one he would pick for her. The trolley was loaded with the entire women's collection.

"I wouldn't want to deprive any piece of jewellery the honour of adorning you. The trolley is yours. Here's my card. Swipe it," Paul turned to get his wallet from the side shelf and handed Glenda his black Amex card.

Glenda stood with her mouth agape. Was she dreaming? Did she hear him correctly? Did he want to buy the entire trolley for her? That would be worth a few thousand dollars. She stood still, blinking with confusion.

"The ... the whole trolley?" were the only words she could come up with after a long pause.

"You want to buy me the whole trolley?" she repeated in disbelief.

Paul smiled and watched her intently. Her reaction to his gesture was worth his share of entertainment for the day.

"Yes," he whispered, his eyes widening with amusement.

Glenda almost fainted with excitement. She could not believe her luck. She would be the proud owner of the entire women's collection from the duty-free catalogue. She held his Amex card tight. She dragged the trolley back, bumping into the other seat clumsily and finally hid herself behind the curtain in the galley.

Glenda was reeling with euphoria. She held Cathy and just kept staring at her. Cathy had heard the conversation. She burned with envy.

Paul looked out of the window. He could imagine with precision the discussion in the service galley. He could perceive Glenda getting ready for the big pay-off. He knew she would take the next few days off to show off her latest possessions.

All this want and all this need—it suffocated him, but he understood it in other people. It seemed to make them happy. And that seemed to make him happy.

He had been looking for something, for someone. It felt like he was trying to find himself. It seemed to him that there was more to him than he knew; there was more to him than he had become. He had been looking for something—a void that he couldn't explain or fill, for he seemed perfectly at ease when he had it—nothing. Or maybe it was old age that was showing its grey and muddled head.

Glenda returned with a bottle of Glenfiddich.

"This one is not on the bill," she smiled a submissive smile as she handed back the black card to Paul. She half expected him to grab her hand and pin her onto the seat next to him. She still was floating on a pink cloud with her bag full of gifts, but was focused on serving Paul in accordance of his expectation from her.

"Who is the pilot today?" Paul posed the surprise question.

"Huh?" Glenda straightened up. What kind of question was that? It was so out of context of the seduction game that seemed to be going on between them. Something was up with Paul. She sensed it. Or maybe he was only asking to check if someone he knew was in the cockpit.

"Captain Robert and First Officer Tom," Glenda tried to re-orient herself, pulling herself out of the cloud that she was floating on.

Paul narrowed his eyes and then shrugged.

"Get me a bottle of water," Paul said distractedly. Glenda darted in and out of the galley, ready in wait for his service.

"I'm going to take a walk," Paul got up from his seat, flung the side of his cabin open and stood next to Glenda, whose heart was doing a double beat. Gifts or no gifts, she found Paul irresistibly attractive.

"Yeah, sure," Glenda stretched out her hand making way for him. The first class cabin was the smallest section of the aircraft. He would do rounds like a goldfish and then bore himself to sleep. She smiled at that thought.

Paul opened the curtain that sealed off the section. "I'm going to take a walk across the aircraft. How long is it?" he asked, stretching his hands out.

"138 feet," an alarmed Glenda declared. Why was he going away? Did he not want a favour in return for all the gifts he had showered on her? Or maybe he would come back for her after the walk? Maybe it was gas. She was confused.

Paul would come back. However, he would not come back for Glenda. Giving in return for nothing was his latest indulgence.

Paul stepped off his lofty abode, entering into the world where every other person would give everything they had to have everything he had. He entered into a world where most people would be delighted to trade their own identity with his. And Paul, on the other hand, would happily give it all up, all he had, so he could have what he hadn't—the chance to be his true self.

THE POINT OF NO RETURN

The moon shone shyly in the greyish blue sky. The setting was surreal as were the events that were unfolding in the sky. The stars were fast receding into their slumber, fading away from view. A land of clouds was sailing below. No life existed in the space which held, on one side, a life locked up in the rules of the planet and, on the other side, a world of freedom which only a few dared to traverse.

Tom's stomach held half the contents of his spiked coffee. The cup sat on the tray, half empty—or as one would optimistically say—half full. The cells in his stomach went into mutiny with the first impact of the poison. His stomach muscles contracted into a cramp in an attempt to haul the coffee back out of his body. Tom held his stomach tight and sighed with a sudden and sharp pain. The poison was acting fast.

Robert tried to keep a straight face, with no interest whatsoever in Tom's discomfort.

"I shouldn't have had that coffee on an empty stomach," Tom muttered and buzzed for the flight attendant.

Robert turned to grab his cup of coffee and his face turned a shade of grey as he looked at the tray. The tray on his side was empty and the coffee sat neatly on the holder in Tom's armrest. He kept staring at the tray. There was a cup on the left towards Tom's side. Tom had picked up Robert's coffee cup.

"Y-y-you," Robert began to fumble with his words. Tom was

startled as Robert's face turned a pale white.

"You drank my coffee!" Robert whispered as his gut sank into his feet.

A confused Tom stared at his coffee cup, not knowing what Robert was getting at. He then bent over and looked at the tray. He had taken the cup on Robert's side, for his cup sat pretty to the left of the tray.

"I-I'm sorry, Captain. I didn't realize ... I was looking at my phone. I picked up your cup by mistake. Darn, these seats in the cockpit are so close together." Tom eyed Robert cautiously. *Why was he overreacting and throwing such a fit over a cup of coffee?*

"You drank my coffee!" Robert roared at first with anger and then settled into fright. He turned to face Tom as his hands reached out to the cup in his armrest. He yanked the cup out and slammed it on the tray.

"What have you done?" his voice quivered, his breath storming in his lungs. "What have you done!" he said furiously.

"You have another vitamin, right?" Tom tried to smile, not sure of Robert's further reaction.

Robert picked up the half empty coffee cup and kept staring at it. He wanted to go back in time and undo the error. He thought hard, fighting a blindness that was hitting his eyes with a black darkness. He *had* kept his cup on his side. Tom had certainly taken his cup of coffee, the coffee that would lead him to his certain death, very soon.

"I'm sorry, Captain," Tom tried to keep his speech steady for a lisp was building up in his talk.

Robert was devastated. He had dived into an imaginary pit of extreme fear. What had he done? What had Tom done!! He needed to think fast. He had wanted to die, and he didn't want to die alone. In his warped state of planning, he had decided to kill himself while in air. He had thought through his plans to end his own life, but killing someone else had not been on his agenda. This plot had moved a level up from suicide. It had moved to murder.

Cathy knocked and entered the cockpit. One look at Tom and her brows creased into a worry.

"Get me something to eat," Tom forced a smile.

Cathy smiled with a hint of concern and picked up the tray.

"You haven't touched your coffee," she scowled at Robert. "Would you like another one?"

Robert was tongue-tied. His legs were shaking and he tried to steady them by placing his hands on his thighs. Beads of sweat shone on his forehead. He heard Cathy speak, but he did not hear what she said. What had he done? His hand shook as he placed it on his forehead nervously. He ran his hand over his sweaty skin and then pulled it down to wipe it on his shirt. He felt for the second capsule in his chest pocket. He had just committed murder. Tom would be dead soon.

What should he do now? Should he take the second capsule immediately and end it all? But that would take three hundred people to their end too. Should he save them all and then serve a life sentence in jail? Two options stood before him—a choice he had to make in the next few seconds—die alone in jail, or die along with the plane full of people.

Energy is infectious. It pervades everything it touches. Just like a person with a positive vibe has a positive impact on people around him with his presence, so too does a negative person. Even when they don't mean harm to you, negative people, with their mere energy, infect you with their negativity. And like an idle housefly, you are caught in their sinister web of destruction.

Cathy stood studying the two men. She had never seen two characters that baffled her more—one was in pain, the other in oblivion. Captain Robert had not even replied to her question about the coffee. She took the silence as a cue and dashed out of the cockpit. She wanted to tell Glenda that something was terribly wrong, but Glenda was too distracted with her bagful of gifts.

"Maybe I will get Captain Joe to fill in if I don't feel better after the meal," Tom complained.

"Hey, Captain," Tom turned to Robert and let out a laugh. "You gotta loosen up man," he started to laugh uncontrollably. The poison had attacked his cells and was now hijacking the operations to lead the body to its sinister purpose—death.

"I wanted to let you know that we all admire you. You are the most admirable captain the airline has. What you do and what you stand for demands courage that a whole plane full of people cannot match up to," Tom said. His speech had begun to slur a bit now.

"I speak highly of you to my colleagues. I think of you often when I am feeling low. It's not easy to volunteer for war, knowing you may not make it back. It's not easy to be in the face of the enemy, knowing you could be mutilated for life. It's not easy to witness the loss of your friends and family. Yet you continued to serve and fulfil your purpose. Anyone else in your shoes would have broken down long ago," Tom held Robert's shoulder tight.

Don't say this. Don't say this now, Robert's voice screamed inside his head. *Why do people tell you good things in the end? Why does everyone save the best for the last? Had Tom said this at the beginning of the flight rather than mocking him, it would have saved many lives, including his own.*

Robert picked up the coffee cup and held it tight in his hand. Tom had consumed half the cup. Even two sips would have done the job. Half a cup was more than enough. Tom's death was certain. The poison would not fail in its promise. Regret began to raise its ugly head in Robert's heart.

What should I do now? What can I do now? Robert's stomach churned with anxiety. His actions had taken him to a point of no return with his plan. The time forward only marked a countdown to the end—Tom's, his own, and potentially that of three hundred others.

Tom raised his hand to wipe the saliva that had begun to drool out of his mouth. His hand shook and he was finding it difficult to keep his head straight. His eyes were beginning to water. The controls on the cockpit were beginning to blur.

"Was that Vitamin C, Captain? I don't feel healthy as you had promised," Tom started on another bout of laughter, his saliva drooling further.

Robert's head was racing at the speed of light. *What should I do now?* No answer befitting decency came up in his mind. His hand reached out and switched off the radio control. Anything said or done here onward would never reach the receiver on land.

The numbers clicked on the lock to the cockpit, and Robert's heart sank into his feet as Cathy made her infamous appearance with a tray of salad and soup for Tom.

The sunglasses on Tom's face hid his watery and glassy eyes. He tried to turn in Cathy's direction, but he seemed to be losing all muscular control.

"Please put the tray down quickly. I am switching on the seat belt sign. There is turbulence ahead," Robert said urgently.

"You didn't touch your coffee," Cathy commented. She left that cup in place and cleared the half empty coffee cup from the tray, the contents of which were quickly transporting Tom to the end of his time. Cathy glanced at Tom, who sat uncomfortably still and quiet, very unlike himself.

"Okay then," Cathy muttered, her tone reflecting a vibe of distrust as she darted out of the cabin.

Something was seriously weird. Cathy had picked up on the vibe. She was tuned into the future.

*****

"Come in," Captain Joe shouted as he heard a knock on the cabin door.

Cathy entered the crew rest cabin. Joe was all snuggled into the reclined seat with his eye mask resting on his forehead. He had decided to catch a nap and then get into the cockpit to relieve the captain.

"There is something I need to talk to you about," Cathy said nervously.

"Sure. Before we get to it, could you get me a cup of coffee please?" Joe smiled sleepily. Joe was quite an indifferent personality. He was used to the gossip of the flight attendants, about the captains or other flight attendants and he couldn't care less. He was putting in his flying hours and doing his job as a rote mechanism with no real interest or passion for his work. He knew the checks were done correctly before takeoff and he knew that qualified captains were in the cockpit. That was all he needed to know to switch off from responsibility and take a break while his rest time lasted.

Cathy slipped out of the cabin and caught Glenda's arm.

"A coffee for Captain Joe, please," she passed the order on and went back to the resting cabin.

Glenda had just been promoted to being a billionaire's indulgence and didn't like the order that Cathy had put her way. Why couldn't she make the coffee? What was her hurry? Captain Joe was resting, so why did she have to go into his cabin? Was she trying to get one up above her by getting busy with the captain, so she could prove her desirability?

"Tsk. Tsk." Glenda muttered to herself. "How desperate," she said inaudibly.

She stood at the counter and saw the half-filled coffee cup that Cathy had brought out from the cockpit. Glenda smiled and poured in fresh hot coffee to fill up the old cup, a distasteful action that had become a habit with her. *'Why waste a good brew?'* was her rationale every time she did that. Waiting on others and serving them was obviously not her purpose.

"I have a feeling something is wrong," Cathy hushed.

Joe sighed. He had heard this before. He did not like playing counsellor thirty-five thousand feet above the planet.

"What happened?" Joe asked, faking concern.

"It's Captain Tom. I think something's wrong with him," Cathy expressed her worry.

Joe sighed. Captain Tom was not like the other captains. He was not someone who would sleep around and was faithful to his girlfriend. His behaviour sometimes annoyed the women who took a fancy to him because, sometimes, pretty women don't take rejection very gracefully.

"Coffee for you, Captain," Glenda butted in, disrupting their conversation. She eyed Cathy rather coldly, pulled out the tray from the seat arm and placed the coffee cup with a napkin and a plate of cookies. She paused for a second, casting a quick glance at the two and then made her way out of the cabin.

"Is everything okay with her?" Joe smiled, bringing the coffee to his lips as the remnants of the hemlock and aconite swirled in the cup ready for their next prey.

Captain Joe was obviously not taking Cathy's worry and concern about Tom seriously. She couldn't express what she sensed and Joe mistook it for idle gossip. They both were obviously not on the same page. How could Captain Joe, ever in his wildest dreams, have an idea of what was going on in the cockpit? How could Cathy ever decipher how to put into words what she felt intuitively in her mind—that Tom was not his usual self and that she smelled trouble, grave trouble ahead?

Captain Joe had changed the topic and Cathy took that as a sign of his disinterest. She abandoned her attempt to explain to Joe that something was terribly wrong in the cockpit. She politely left the cabin.

When people don't acknowledge their perceptions and when they don't give credit to their intuitive abilities, they relinquish their power. They see the future and then pretend that they didn't see it. They know the truth and then pretend they don't know it. They feel, they sense, they estimate, and then they turn around and seek approval for their evaluations.

The future was perceived, and the future was invalidated.

The present was heading towards an irreversible destiny because one person couldn't handle his senses. Another person, who sensed the danger of the situation, couldn't communicate it assertively, and yet another who received the communication, evaluated its worth not with present facts but past experiences.

One person was insane, but many others were fuelling the consequence of his insanity.

Cathy would have a chance to learn this lesson, but she may not have a chance to benefit from it.

*****

"Really, I will finish my book?" Sarah was delighted. Her insecurities about Mike and her fatigue from the day's work evaporated with that prediction. A surge of energy hit her. That is the power of hope. That is the power of purpose.

"I am only telling you what the stars are telling me." Muttu was on the verge of falling ill. It was not Sarah's prediction that was troubling him. His life was flashing in front of his eyes at manic speed. His mind was split into two. One half was conversing with Sarah and the other half was dispersed in utter confusion. It was as though he could see that the future held a joke that summed up his own life.

"Actually, I haven't told anyone that I have already written a book. I'm just stuck on the last chapter. It's a love story—a sad love story. When I sent it to my editor, he said that I lacked the depth and understanding of human emotions. And so I stopped writing. One more chapter and the book will be complete," Sarah confessed.

Jim was secretly proud of Sarah. Although he was tuned into his music, each time Sarah spoke, he lowered his volume to hear what she had to say. He wanted to know Sarah better. He had taken a very strong liking to her. Sarah was an author, smart, intelligent, sensitive and incredibly attractive. She seemed to be his 'type', only fifteen years older.

"You will write it," Muttu said softly as he stared at his computer screen. He wasn't looking at the numbers anymore; he was looking at his whole life.

"Can I ask you another question?" Sarah continued despite Muttu's silence. He seemed a little off to her suddenly. He was the one who had started the conversation with her and gotten her interested in his work, and now that she was hooked, he seemed to have lost interest in chatting with her.

"Yeah," Muttu replied, tearing his attention off his own life and looking at Sarah.

Maybe he was tired or maybe he was just sleepy. Sarah tried to justify his behaviour in her head.

"Will my book be published?" Sarah asked, despite her lack of confidence that it ever would be.

"Let me see," Muttu brought his focus back to the present and slowly started to punch in some numbers. Did he really want to see? He knew the answer. But he did what a professional does—follow the process. As he pressed 'enter' some numbers began to rearrange themselves in the eight boxes that held Sarah's destiny.

How does one break bad news to someone? How does someone tell them that the future that they are desperately holding on to, does not exist? Being an astrologer was intriguing but could put one in a dilemma at times. People look up to you for validating their dreams and then you sometimes have to be the bad guy who shatters their dreams.

The woman next to him was going to die in five hours. She was asking him if her dream would be fulfilled. How could he deny her that hope? She had only five hours to live. But then again, how could he lie and be untrue to his profession?

The longer Muttu's silence persisted, the more doubt crept into Sarah's world.

"I guess not," she read Muttu's energy.

"I'm sorry," Muttu mumbled. Jim squirmed in his seat. He wanted to get up and beat Muttu for breaking Sarah's heart with all this astrology mumbo-jumbo.

What a jerk this man is! Jim cursed. *Doesn't he care for people's feelings? Is he God to predict someone's future and destroy their dreams?*

"I think your book will be published," Jim spoke, quite alarmed at his sudden display of courage.

Sarah smiled at Jim's effort to cheer her up.

"I'm Jim, by the way," he turned left to face Sarah and then shot a stern glance at Muttu. Muttu was quite introverted and missed Jim's threatening glare.

"You should complete your book. And send it out. If no one takes it, then maybe it's not their time yet to be a part of your purpose. But don't quit." Jim spoke loudly at first, but then realizing that most of the other passengers were asleep, lowered his volume.

"I play soccer. I had a knee injury a couple of months ago. My coach told me that I would not make it, that I was not as fast as I should be in the game. I was not selected for the team and I came to Dubai with my parents on a holiday. Yesterday, I got an email from my coach that I was in," Jim tried his best to instil back the hope in Sarah's dream, which Muttu had stolen with his stupid prediction.

"I didn't ask the coach why he changed his mind. It wasn't he who had changed his mind, it was *I* who had *not* changed my mind about the game. I didn't give up. I knew I would be in the game. My fate was not for the coach to decide. I had already decided it."

"Who's to say?" Jim was ready to pick a fight with Muttu. He was ready to argue with him for the next fourteen hours if needed, to protect Sarah and her dreams. Such an emotional attachment with a stranger who was way out of his league and such an emotional repulsion towards a person whom he had just met, alarmed Jim.

"Yeah. That's true." The startled trio looked up at the man who had been eavesdropping on their conversation.

"We make our own destiny. I believe that."

Jim was delighted to have an ally in a complete stranger who stood mysteriously in the dark.

*****

"I need help," Tom whispered.

His head was hanging low. A long trail of saliva was dripping from his mouth. The buttons on the cockpit were circling in his vision. A feeling of numbness was fast consuming him.

"Something's happening to me," he slurred.

Robert looked at him, his breathing now rapid and heavy. *What should I do?* The question echoed in his head with deafening volume. From suicide to murder, this plan had gone seriously wrong.

Tom tried to lift himself up from the chair but his body just lunged forward and his arms fell feebly on the control panel. Robert leapt off his chair to hold him back to ensure the controls did not get messed up.

Robert held Tom in his seat with one hand and with the other hand he turned on the seat belt sign. He pressed the call button and waited for a flight attendant to answer the call. Tom stared at Robert, a froth now building in the corners of his mouth.

"Yes, Captain?" Cathy answered the phone.

"Please return to your seats. We are expecting some turbulence," Robert spoke urgently into the speaker.

"It was you," Tom said, looking at Robert with disbelief. He was losing control of his head. It was drooping and jerking in any direction that the weight carried it.

"You ... you poisoned the coffee," he whispered. Even though his body controls were failing, he could decipher Robert's involvement in his condition because of his indifference towards his sickness. Why wasn't he helping him? Why did he want to kill him?

Tom was alive and was confronting Robert with the truth. Robert didn't know how to react. He couldn't deny his doing and he couldn't lie about it. He was holding Tom captive in the cockpit, and that made his intention clear.

"Why? Robert, why?" Tom begged. Everything was happening so fast that he just couldn't make any sense of it. Why would Robert want to kill him? He couldn't come up with one justified reason or even one insane excuse. He had done nothing to harm Robert. He was just an ordinary pilot. He had no special achievements that Robert could be jealous of. He had no special assets that Robert might want to get out of him. It didn't make sense.

"Why?" He begged again for an answer. Tom was gathering every bit of will power to fight the numbness that was growing in his head to turn his eyes in Robert's direction and face him.

"I wanted to kill myself. The poison was for me. I *want* to die," Robert held his face in his hands. "That coffee was for me. I wanted to die here, at work. I wanted to go in peace. But you drank my coffee, you fool. I didn't want you to die; I wanted to kill myself," he let out a sob.

Although Tom couldn't understand it, he knew that Robert was telling the truth. Insanity has no explanation and trying to explain it is as futile as trying to understand it.

"Am I going to *die*?" Tom whispered. He was trying desperately to take control of the situation, to somehow save his life. He attempted again to lunge forward and only fell onto his right, pushing the throttle down, tilting the entire plane.

"Oh my freaking God," Robert yelped, as the plane took a sharp nosedive. He leapt at the throttle bringing it back into position, steadying the aircraft. He had to do something about Tom. He was losing control and he was going to wreak havoc. He needed to be stopped.

Robert bent down and opened up the laces of his shoes and pulled them out. Tears began to well up in his eyes. He was face to face with the death he had so dearly wished for himself. He was a witness to the process of dying he had so carefully constructed in his head. However, what was happening right now was nowhere close to his endless hours of preparation for death. Watching someone else die a death he had planned for himself took away the urge to die. Robert trembled as he got up and held Tom against the seat, tying his arms on the armrest with his laces.

"Am I going to die?" Tom slurred and then moaned.

"Yes," Robert held his face by the chin and then pushed his

head back. His look was stern, like a Major on a mission. "We are all going to die, if that is any solace."

*****

The Air Traffic Control had lost all radio contact with SL502. This was the longest that there had been no signal. The plane was on its course as detected on the radar. The chief called in through the satellite service. The phone buzzed in the service galley.

"Put me to the captain. We don't have radio contact," the voice cracked over the phone. The blood from Cathy's face drained. She *knew* it. She knew something was wrong. Her hand began to tremble as she held the reciever.

"Let me connect you to the captain," she said, buzzing the resting cabin instead of connecting the line to the cockpit. She did not trust the two captains in charge of the plane; she wanted Joe to hear it from someone else and figure out the situation. She had tried to explain her intuition to him, but failed. Maybe the call from ATC would put the situation in perspective for him.

"Hello," Joe answered on the remote phone. A strange numbness was taking over. *I need to sleep it off and put a Do Not Disturb outside my cabin,* he thought to himself. He needed to leave the affairs of the captains and the flight attendants for them to resolve. Although Cathy had complained that she felt there was something fishy happening in the cockpit and that she had a bad feeling about it, Joe had promised to take over in half an hour after a short nap. It had only been a few minutes and here she was buzzing him again.

"It's the ATC; they are calling from the ground. The radio on the flight is off. They can't make contact with the cockpit," Cathy spoke urgently. Glenda picked up on the uneasiness.

"Put them through," Joe tried to sit upright but only collapsed back in his seat. What was happening?

"General Catsner from ATC. What's wrong, Captain? We can't make radio contact with the cockpit," the head of ATC barked at the other end of the line.

Shit, Joe thought. The General had assumed that Joe was in the cockpit.

"Give me a minute, General. I will report the problem," Joe tried his best to sound in control, but the slur in his voice not only startled him but alarmed the General as well.

"Are you all right, Captain?" His voice was slow and loaded with alertness.

Something was wrong. He could pick it up from the tone. The call, which should have been directed to the captain in charge of the plane, had been transferred to the captain off work. The General signalled to the ground staff and they all tuned in to the call.

"Yes, I'm fine. I was resting. Let me check with the cockpit and revert to you," Joe tried desperately to get up but he couldn't. His head spun, and the receiver slipped out of his hand.

"Captain! Captain!" The voice yelled on the other end. "The line is still active. Keep it active," the General barked instructions to the men at ground control.

Joe had slumped back into his seat involuntarily. He felt paralyzed as though some force was pushing him down against his will. What was happening?

"Help," he spoke between heavy breaths.

"SL502 is being hijacked!" General Catsner barked into his walkie-talkie, bringing the authorities at Air Traffic Control at Dubai International Airport to a screeching halt.

*****

Glenda turned around and grabbed the phone. It buzzed nervously in the cockpit. The seat belt sign was still turned on. Robert picked up the phone and waited for a flight attendant to speak.

"Captain, Air Traffic Control called. The radio is turned off. Is everything all right?" Glenda was a little troubled now. She had been flying for six years now and she knew that a call from the ground meant trouble.

"Shit," Robert muttered inaudibly. He had forgotten all about the satellite phone. This was not all part of his original plan. He had only wanted to kill himself. This whole business with Tom had taken him on a path of crime. He was not used to thinking like a criminal. He was now torn between being a man with suicidal tendencies and a man who was en route to becoming an avowed criminal.

"Yeah. Everything is fine." Robert stretched his hand out and switched off the connection to the satellite phone. He looked at Tom who was frothing at the mouth. The heaving of his chest and the occasional blinking of his eyes showed that he was still alive.

"Let me check on the radio. It seems fine to me. I will send a signal back," Robert said, faking control, while his stomach was fast sinking into his knees. "Er, who took the call from ATC?" Robert asked, his hands shaking on the controls.

"Captain Joe," Glenda said.

Robert was sweating profusely. His mind was racing in all directions. He quickly put a lock on the door. He punched in a few codes, which would not allow the door to be opened from the outside. ATC had reached the aircraft; Captain Joe had taken the call. The cat would be out of the bag soon. This was bad news for him.

Three minutes passed. With every passing second, Robert expected a pounding on the door or for the phone to ring. His heart was in his mouth, awaiting the mayhem that would soon erupt. Strangely, nothing happened. There was silence. Where was Joe? He had taken the call from ATC. He should have been here the very next second. Something was wrong.

Cathy got up and punched the numbers to the cockpit door. She needed to know what the hell was going on. She was going to make an entrance without permission. The red light on the combination lock stayed on. That was strange. She punched the numbers again. It was locked. The code had been changed.

Robert stared at the door. He had to do something fast.

The radio was cut off. He also cut off all wireless and satellite connections. Now no one could send a message from the plane or make contact with it. He turned the plane forty-degrees, taking a sharp turn back.

✳✳✳✳✳

The plane tipped to one side as it bent into a turn and the flight attendants made an urgent announcement asking all passengers to be seated with their seat belts tightly fastened.

Paul swayed to the right, losing his balance. Standing in the aisle of the economy class, engrossed in a conversation about destiny and fate with a teenager and an astrologer from the spiritual land of India was a better indulgence for him than entertaining the seductively enthusiastic flight attendant in first class. With Sarah being the damsel in question, Paul was enjoying himself.

Paul was a long way from the first class section when the seat belt sign flashed on. Muttu reluctantly offered him the empty seat next to him.

"Are we taking a turn?" Paul asked the question to no one in particular, as he stared out the window. The same question troubled the flight crew, a move which alerted them all that there was trouble in the cockpit.

Paul was a frequent flier and knew what most sounds and turns of the aircraft meant. He narrowed his brows. The plane was certainly making a turn, which was rather odd. As per his experience, an aircraft always flew straight to its destination. The turns came at landing, not in the journey.

Paul flicked on the TV screen. The flight path was a static screen showing no change, no movement. That was odd. He looked at Muttu and then looked away, trying hard to figure what was happening. When he would return to his seat, he would demand a word with the captain.

Paul looked out of the window. He had forgotten the feel of travelling in economy. The seat was too small. The arrangement seemed quite like the arrangement in prison to him, too many people in too little space. The only common factor between economy and first class was the window size. No matter where you are, the window is a common place of opportunity. Paul smiled at that thought.

The sky had turned baby blue and the clouds were catching a hint of orange, announcing the arrival of the sun.

"Why did you choose to be an astrologer?" Paul turned to Muttu. The entire row of 26 was wide awake, while most of the passengers were fast asleep. "It must be quite difficult," Paul empathized with Muttu. "Isn't destiny best left to be discovered?"

"I didn't choose it. My profession chose me," Muttu confessed. "The future is a result of what you do in the present and what you have done in the past. But what you also need to know is that the future is also a result of what others do in the present in your environment."

Paul narrowed his brows, prompting Muttu to explain.

"Let's say you are a successful businessman. You are doing everything right and everything is in order. Now one of your trusted people back-stabs you and brings your company down. So then, your destiny of despair was not your own doing, really. It was the doing of another person who was a part of your world. We tend to think that our actions alone count in the larger scheme of things. That's only half the truth. It is also true that we are impacted by the actions of those around us. You could be driving on a highway on your side of the road. You don't drink. You have checked your car. In addition, you have taken every responsible action that you possibly could have, to ensure your safety. Then a drunk driver gets into your lane, throwing you off into a ravine. Our destinies are intertwined. If I am in your space now, my karma impacts you and your future," Muttu explained to Paul, who was utterly baffled by this logic.

Jim was a bit quiet too. He had already argued enough with Muttu and had reached a space of calm where he could see his logic.

"So what can you tell?" Paul asked Muttu, a question he had heard a million times in his career.

"Almost everything," Muttu said, uninterested.

"I have a question that I have always wondered about," Paul spoke softly. He didn't want Sarah and Jim listening in.

The plane dipped suddenly. Paul gripped the seat tight as Muttu's laptop slid off the tray. He caught it just in time before it hit the floor.

"Shit!" Jim screeched loudly.

"Oh God. Oh God." Sarah leaned onto Jim, who immediately held her hand protectively.

"It's okay. Just some turbulence," he consoled her.

Those who had been yanked out of their slumber waited anxiously for an apology or announcement from the pilot. There was none. The flight attendant took over the responsibility.

"Ladies and gentlemen. We are experiencing some turbulence. Please remain seated and keep your seat belts tightly fastened."

"It happens when the aircraft enters an air pocket. There is nothing to worry," Jim reassured a worried Sarah.

I should not have taken this flight. Serves me right for suspecting Mike, Sarah cursed herself.

Paul had forgotten all about his question and he was trying to make sense of what was going on. The plane had made a sharp turn, which wasn't normal on a long-haul flight. And then the dip. He had taken enough flights to understand the laws of aviation. It was Muttu who broke into his thoughts. Not that Muttu was interested in giving Paul a reading, but he was interested in taking his mind off the negative energy that was looming in the air.

"What did you want to ask?" Muttu broke the gloomy silence.

Why isn't the pilot speaking up? Paul turned his thoughts out and looked at Muttu.

"Well, I have spent the most part of my life creating and building a dream that I have been living since the last decade. I thought that when I would have money, I would be happy. I thought that if I created an empire, I would be successful. And I have been both, happy and successful. I have won more than I have lost. I have been high more than I have been low. I have had troubles and then I have had my abundant share of victories. I have everything that I had dreamed I would ever have. My children and their next three generations are covered financially. I have everything," Paul paused to catch his breath, speaking as softly as possible.

"But why then do I feel this void, as if I have missed out on something. Why do I feel that everything that I have done has been out of alignment with my purpose? Why do I feel that there is more to life than what I have lived? Why do I sometimes think about dying? I am not depressed, but then why do I sometimes think about death as liberation? I am curious. Do you understand what I am talking about?" Paul raised his eyebrows.

This was an awkward conversation for Paul, firstly, because he had never discussed this with anyone and, secondly, because he had never thought it through. Somehow, while hearing Muttu speak, he had this feeling that Muttu would understand. He glimpsed into people's lives and understood them. A man who tells the future bears the burden of their lives too.

"I know what you are saying. I totally do," Muttu was amazed at Paul's spiritual depth, although Paul wouldn't have suspected that he even had a spiritual edge.

"Nothing interests me. I have done everything I could have. I have created everything I could have. I have loved and lost, and I love still. Nothing interests me. There is no challenge that stimulates me anymore. It's like I have been on the ride for so long that I want to get off the ride.

"And lately, I have visions and I have concerns. I can see through people and their intentions. I can predict circumstances; I can see what will happen next. I'm not trying to do it, but it comes to me. I don't have an agenda with what I can see. I don't have a motive. It's just a state, as though I have become an observer of life, not a participant.

"I don't feel any attachment, either to things or to people. Although I go to work every day, and create some magical accomplishments, I care less about that. I create and then I give it away with the same ease. Do you understand what I am saying?" Paul confirmed. His thoughts were so loaded with a spiritual concern that he wondered if anyone had ever felt the way he did.

"I understand you. I know exactly what you mean," Muttu reassured him.

"You do?" Paul didn't mean that to be a question.

"So my question is," Paul hesitated as his voice dropped a few more decibels, so that Muttu had to lean in to hear him, "can you tell me when I will die?"

*****

Where was Joe? Something had happened to him back there. *What could have happened?* There seemed no befitting explanation for his absence from the scene. He would have felt the detour. He would have felt the drop. These were signs of mutiny and Joe had not turned up. Robert couldn't think straight anymore.

The monitor kept beeping that the aircraft was off track. This was a dangerous ride, as it could potentially get in the way of other aircraft leading to a collision. It was too late to get back on track, as Robert had cut off all signals to the ground. The plane was tuned into the compass and getting it back on track would only be an inaccurate estimate.

There was an aircraft that was flying in with the rising sun as its backdrop. That collision would take a toll of six hundred lives. Robert pushed the aircraft to an abrupt drop.

Dark clouds loomed below, as the aircraft began to quickly lose altitude. The radar showed three red dots. These red dots are always a source of worry to pilots. They indicate heavily charged clouds that are alive with an electric force. An aircraft must steer clear of the region for, sometimes, even the periphery is charged with enough electric force to cause significant turbulence, and sometimes even electronic failure.

The aircraft was dropping down now close to twenty thousand

feet, and the dark spread was floating below, waiting to swallow the ride of three hundred people to alternate destinies.

Robert had reached his wits' end. He was aimlessly flying the aircraft. Killing Tom had messed up his mind completely. He reached out for the capsule in his pocket and took it out of the plastic sheet. He held it in his hand and reached for the bottle of water. He would swallow the poison and then lead the aircraft into the charged cloud. Hopefully, lightning would strike the fuel tank and cause the aircraft to explode in a second. Or it would damage the controls and the aircraft would lunge to its end. Alternatively, the electric charge could throw the aircraft off control, and it would fall to its inevitable destruction. He would be paralyzed in minutes, and it would end for him before it ended for everyone else.

He unscrewed the bottle. His hands trembled, as did his body. It was the body's rebellion against putting to an end what it had so faithfully worked at keeping alive. The capsule slipped onto his palm and then off his hand onto the floor.

"Darn," he muttered and bent down to look for the capsule that had rolled into a cavity under his seat. His body still shaking, Robert looked around for a thin stick to dislodge the capsule from the cavity.

The red dots were becoming bigger and bigger as the red light began to blink and a warning sound beeped urgently on the radar.

*****

"Why are we losing altitude?" Cathy snapped open her seat belt. Turbulence hit the aircraft as it jerked to the left and then to the right.

"Sit down," Glenda panicked. If the plane dipped once more, Cathy could fall. A fall in the service galley is more dangerous than falling in the passenger aisle.

However, Cathy was not going to sit down. She went to the door of the cockpit and punched in the code again. The red light beeped once more on the lock. She pounded on the door.

"Captain!" she yelled and then put her ear to the door. She heard the alarm beeping in the cockpit and her heart sank into her stomach.

"Captain," she yelled louder pounding the door with her fist. She held onto the walls of the galley because the aircraft had begun to sway.

Cathy looked towards the crew resting cabin. Captain Joe had taken the call from ATC and maybe had communicated with the cockpit. Nevertheless, something seemed fishy. Cathy had expected Captain Joe to come out and get into the cockpit. Why had he not come out? She tried to make her way towards the cabin, but Glenda had got up and caught Cathy by the arm.

"Sit down," Glenda was also worried about the aircraft losing altitude and the captain not responding, but she wanted Cathy to be by her side.

Glenda buzzed the cockpit.

"Stay calm and pray," Robert spoke into the receiver without waiting for Glenda to ask the question and then the line went dead.

"What did he say?" Cathy shook Glenda's arm as the blood drained from her face.

"Stay calm and pray," Glenda whispered.

"Damn you, woman! What did he say?" Cathy shouted, shaking Glenda.

"Stay calm and pray. He said stay calm and pray," Glenda was barely audible.

"I will get Captain Joe," Cathy snapped her seat belt open again and trudged towards the crew resting cabin, despite the turbulence, making every step she took a challenge.

*****

The turbulence had woken everyone up. Even those who were trying to brush it off as 'normal' were now wide awake in their seats, looking at one another for reassurance. Most people managed to keep a straight face, hoping it was only temporary. A couple of men had gotten up demanding to speak to the captain. However, the flight was so turbulent that they had no option but to get back to their seats and hope for the best.

Sarah was breathing heavily. Jim was a little concerned himself. But he kept reassuring Sarah, keeping his enthusiasm high, betting on the probability that the turbulence would pass.

Paul and Muttu were in a different zone. The turbulence was a sign for Muttu, a sign that was loyal to his prediction, to his foresight into the future. Paul was already heading towards his liberation, pushing his urgency to continue his conversation with Muttu.

Muttu was used to all kinds of questions. But it was not very often that someone was curious about his end. Paul seemed like a successful man, a reasonable man. His limited edition

Hublot and his diamond-studded Cartier cufflinks spoke about his success before he even mentioned it.

Successful businessmen, politicians, actors, diplomats, and other people in power had formed Muttu's loyal clientele. He had been asked every question imaginable. He had even been consulted on the most ridiculous of subjects like 'which car should I buy' or 'what deal should I play at the stock market'. However, it was a very rare occasion when a perfectly happy man walked in with a question, 'when am I going to die?'

The question was not a problem. People will ask anything. Whether Muttu should answer, was based on the ethics of his profession—he must not tell about the death of an individual.

"I don't have an answer to that question, Paul. I don't have the answer," he paused, evaluating how badly Paul wanted to know and how he would react if he told him. Paul seemed calm and composed. Even the jerky aircraft was not interfering with his emotions.

"You just said that you could tell anything," Paul reminded Muttu.

"Yes," Muttu nodded. He could tell everything but that.

"Is it that you can't tell because you can't see or you can see, but you won't tell?" Paul searched Muttu's eyes for an answer before he could say it.

"I can see but I cannot tell," Muttu confessed.

Paul went silent. He bit his lip and stared grimly out of the window.

Muttu looked at his watch. The lady on his side had about four hours to live. The aircraft was unstable in the air. The vibe of the moment had Satan's feel. The man next to him was potentially on his last few hours before his time was up. What harm could knowing that cause him now? Death and freedom seemed to have been his interest anyway. What harm could a little violation of his professional vows do at this moment, when, a few hours later, he may not have the profession anymore?

"I cannot tell you the answer," Muttu paused, taking Paul's attention from the dark clouds, and back to him, "but I can teach you the basics of astrology so you can decipher the answer for yourself," Muttu said, asking permission to continue.

Paul was stunned with his reply. His mouth was a little open and his breath stopped in that instant. It took him a few seconds to understand how big a sacrifice Muttu was making on his professional ethics to help him see what he desired most to see.

"Can you teach me how to see the future?" Paul asked, penetrating Muttu's eyes.

Muttu asked him the standard questions about his date of birth, time and place, and then began to punch in the numbers into his computer.

"So you take the numbers and you punch them in this sequence," Muttu turned his laptop so Paul could peep in. "The eight boxes represent, lifespan, fame, wealth, family ..."

Paul was hooked onto every word that Muttu said. Paul was sharp and numbers were his game. He caught on. Technology made the deciphering so simple. The astrologer was only reading what the computer calculated. A computer software and some insight into people's behaviour is about all the qualification needed to be an astrologer. Paul smiled at that thought.

"So now we are set with your numbers. When I press 'enter', they will settle in their respective boxes. You know how to read them, right? You know how to read the eighth box now? That's the box that holds the answer to the lifespan. You got that, right?" Muttu ensured that Paul had understood. Paul nodded in comprehension.

Paul let out a long sigh. This was it, he thought. He stared out of the window and the sight of the dark clouds ahead took his attention away from death to survival.

Paul hit the enter button, which threw all the numbers on the computer screen into a frenzy, with the timer rotating for the numbers to settle into their destined future.

A flash of lightning took his attention away from the computer screen to the sky outside.

Is that lightning? He stuck his face to the window. *Are we heading towards that cloud?* Paul turned to face Muttu in alarm. Only to see the same fear reflected in Muttu's expression as well.

Which question should he bring up first? Paul thought. *Can you see the lightning cloud? Or when am I going to die?* The answer to both seemed intertwined.

Muttu and Paul were silent for a few seconds. As Muttu's glance fell on the window and the dark journey ahead, Paul's eyes were fixed on the computer screen. All the numbers were huddled in one box with his name on the top.

"What does this mean?" Paul asked Muttu, despite knowing what it meant. Muttu had just told him what it meant. Muttu had ensured that he had understood how to read the code if his time was up.

"What does it mean, Muttu? My time is up!" Paul's face changed various shades of red, and then shifted to a greyish white.

"Not yet," Muttu whispered, "you still have four hours to live."

Paul's expression froze on that line. It was as though he had become a marble statue. Muttu stared with concern at Paul's ash-white face set against the dark cloud spewing streaks of lightening.

*****

"Is that lightning? Aren't we flying too low? Are we landing?" Sarah turned towards Muttu's window, with Jim leaning onto her to get a better view.

A soft mayhem had broken out with similar questions being raised, but none being answered. The discomfort and the disturbance were building up. The worry was mounting but had not broken into verbal agitation yet.

Jim was worried but tried to stay in control. He was struck by electricity from Sarah and cared less about the electric energy in the clouds.

"It's nothing to worry about," Jim reassured her. "Most aircraft are resistant to lightning," he explained, leaving out the exceptions to the theory. It was true that aircraft were built with conductors resistant to lightning, but that only depended on where the lightning struck and how much power it had. It was not often, but lightning could not only strike an aircraft, but also pass through it, cooking to ash anybody that came in its way.

The descent had bothered Jim and the headway into the clouds looked a little worrisome, but surely the pilot knew what he was doing. His life was at stake too. With that, he let his worries rest.

*****

The turbulence was getting tighter and nastier as Cathy inched her way forward to the resting cabin. Glenda was on the verge of breaking into tears. It was not the turbulence that was creating the panic; it was the pilot's non-responsiveness that told her that something was terribly wrong in the cockpit. When activities in the cockpit go into doubt, then the life and future of everyone on board becomes a question mark. Glenda buzzed the cockpit again. What was going on? Why was Robert not saying anything?

"What is going on?" she begged as Robert answered the receiver. "Why are we descending?"

"I'm sorry," said Robert and hung up. He had left his seat and was aggressively trying to dig into the cavity that held the capsule in place. If he could just get the damn capsule out, it would all be over.

Glenda had begun to sob hysterically. She started to pray. She would return all the gifts that Paul gave her. She would change her karma. She would quit flying and stay on the ground to serve her family. Flying didn't give her the joy that meeting interesting men did. Maybe that's why she was here; maybe that's why she deserved to die. She begged for one more chance, one last chance to live. She buzzed the captain again. Her life was in his hands. The line had gone dead. Robert had put the receiver off its socket.

Cathy saw the lightning and headed quickly to the window. She held the door tightly as she watched with horror the cloud light up, as the lightning ran through it, cutting it in half. Her husband was a pilot and she knew what fate lay for an aircraft that ventured into the dark cloud that appeared as a red warning on the radar. *She had to get to Captain Joe.*

The plane jerked feverishly and a loose trolley rolled towards Cathy smashing into her and holding her in place at the door. It had turned in and lodged sideways from wall to wall. Glenda watched as her sobs now became audible.

"Get to Captain Joe," Cathy yelled despite her state of despair, and a petrified Glenda only held tightly to her seat belt.

*****

The tension was building up among the passengers. Everyone was on the edge of fear, but no one said anything yet. There were murmurs and soft cries and there were reassurances. Everyone was hanging onto the thin rope of hope that the bad weather and the turbulence would pass.

Row 26 had a different story. Paul stared at Muttu, waiting for him to start laughing, saying his prediction was a joke. Muttu looked serious, like a man who was about to die.

"You are messing with me, right?" Paul let out a nervous laugh. "You are testing me, right?" Paul searched Muttu's eyes desperately for a mocking bout of laughter.

Muttu shut his laptop, rubbed his eyes and looked at Paul. Although Muttu's skin was dark, Paul could swear that his face looked a pale shade of yellow.

"Are you all right?" Paul asked, concerned.

"You have four hours to live. That's not the concern. I have seen the end for many in my lifetime. However, the lady next to us has four hours to live too," Muttu gasped for breath.

Paul stared at Muttu in horror. Was he implying that it was a rare twist of coincidence, where two random strangers on a flight were bound with the same destiny or was he implying that the plane was about to crash, leaving two hundred and ninety-three survivors or worse, none?

"What does your destiny say?" Paul asked. His stomach was churning, threatening to pop out of his mouth.

"I cannot see my destiny," Muttu confessed. He never had to see it. He knew it.

"Then see his," Paul pointed to Jim. "Why would two strangers have the same hour of death? Why?" Paul's tone became loud and urgent and then he settled in his seat.

Muttu was sick with concern. He did not need Jim as a confirmation of the future that he could see very clearly without consulting the numbers. He could see the future but hoped desperately that he was wrong.

"Hey, buddy," Paul called out to Jim. The tone of his voice had the desperate feel of trying to stay in control. "What's your date of birth?" he smiled, hoping Jim would comply for some fate-related fun.

"Let's test Muttu with your past to see if what he predicted about my future is correct," Paul invited Jim to play along.

"Huh?" Jim leaned forward. The smell of Sarah's perfume hit his nostrils as he leaned closer. A conversation with Paul would give him the proximity with his crush.

The turbulence was getting nastier and his co-passenger was consulting an astrologer. Jim could sense the wave of desperation in Paul's voice. They were thirty thousand feet in the raging sky—prayer seemed to be the natural response to the potential disaster ahead, and Paul was engaging an astrologer to read his future? Jim was aghast.

"Where I came from is irrelevant," Jim leaned over facing Paul, "but we all seem to be headed towards the same future," he said, pointing to Paul's window at the dark cloud that was growing bigger and bigger every second.

"Why are we headed into the lightning?" Sarah interrupted. Her voice was choked.

"Can you tell if everything will be okay?" She looked at Muttu for reassurance.

"If everything would not be okay, why would he take the flight?" Jim slid closer to Sarah. "He can see the future, right? Why would he take the flight if he saw it as his end?" Jim started to laugh nervously, not taking his eyes off Muttu, whose expression was set in ice.

"Tell him your date of birth," Sarah coaxed Jim. "It would be fun to see what he tells you."

"You mean he should tell me about my past, so we know if he

is authentic in his prediction for the guy there?" Jim faked a smile. Muttu was solemn, in deep thought, and it made Jim nervous. He was mentally trying to connect the dots in his own naïve way to get the drift of the future that lay ahead.

"Yeah," Paul was relieved that he had bought his bait. "What's your date of birth?"

"6th December 1991," Jim lied. It was better to be nineteen than seventeen. The message was for Sarah.

Muttu took that as a cue and, without being asked, began to punch in the numbers on his laptop.

Paul was fighting bouts of nausea as his eyes were glued to Muttu's computer screen. He knew nothing about the alignment of numbers, but he had just learned to identify the pattern of death.

The numbers fanned out beautifully, lodging themselves randomly in the eight boxes that held a fate that did not belong to Jim. Muttu wiped the sweat from his forehead. "You have a long life," he laughed out loud in Jim's direction.

"He has a long life," Muttu squeezed Paul's hand. If Jim was going to survive then SL502 was not going down, Muttu heaved a sigh of relief.

Paul felt a pull towards Sarah. What was it about him and her that their lives were going to end at the same hour? He wanted to know her. He wanted to speak to her.

"Why are Sarah and I dying at the same time and the same place?" Paul turned to face Muttu. "It's not the timing; it's the proximity as well. That's too much of a coincidence. What is my connection with her?"

"So what are you going to tell me about my life?" Jim interrupted their conversation. He had given his date of birth and was demanding a reading. Sarah was curious too.

In his moment of relief, Muttu had forgotten all about Jim's reading. The aircraft came to his rescue, saving him from indulging in a conversation that would put his ability to ridicule, as Jim's reading would not match that of his life.

The aircraft had begun to shake feverishly as though it had gone into a convulsion. There was a momentary silence and then subdued mutters and then some loud curses.

Jim straightened up and looked at Sarah. He could not bear to see her in discomfort. She looked at him nervously, trying to fake a smile, hiding the terror that was seeping in through her body.

Paul looked at his watch. If he had four hours to live, the plane would make it through the black cloud. Muttu and Paul were the only two calm people on the flight. As the plane lunged forward jerkily, Paul laughed out loud, "Four hours! I have spent forty-six years living, and now I have four hours to die."

*****

The dark grey cloud stood like a wall in the sky. Flashes of lightning threw electric streaks in the direction of the aircraft, like the flickering tongue of a hungry snake. Robert stared ahead, petrified. He was losing his mind. He had to die. He just had to think of how. He didn't want to crash the flight and be responsible for mass murder. Instead, he thought, taking the plane into the thundercloud would rid him of that responsibility, for it would be the natural calamity that would kill them all. Tom was very still. An occasional movement on his chest suggested he was alive but nearing death soon. The colour of his skin was white now, devoid of blood. His eyes were fixated. Tears welled up and streaked down his cheeks at intervals. The froth on his mouth had dried up, giving him a ghastly look.

"I'm sorry," Robert whispered. "It will all be over soon," he said as he watched the gates of hell open up into a large dark cloud turbulent with lightning.

The aircraft was already shaking violently like the sacrificial lamb, threatening to fall apart. The magnetic field around the thundercloud was alive with electric charge, ready to throw the plane off its balance.

What happens when an aircraft enters a thundercloud? Not many have lived to tell. Those who have, were so disturbed by the energy, that they told contradicting stories. Some spoke of light while others described a penetrating darkness. Some said the aircraft was thrown out of the atmosphere while others said that it dived towards the sea even if none existed on their route. Those who made it out alive were lucky, but their stories were too incredulous to be believed, and they lived the rest of their lives stuck in that thunderstorm.

The beeps grew urgent and louder as the aircraft speedily approached the electric boundary of the blackish grey thundercloud. A whip of lightning lit up the cloud, blinding Robert, welcoming its prey.

*****

The entire aircraft had broken into a frantic din. Gods were being called upon, hands were being held, tears were being shed and fear was running loose in every heart, except on Row 26.

A few people attempted again to get up and go to the cockpit to ask, 'what the hell is going on?' The turbulence and the co-passengers kept them in their seats. People were looking at each other drawing fear or drawing hope from one another's reactions.

Sarah, like everyone else, was shaking in her seat as the plane shook incessantly.

"You are nineteen?" Sarah tried to engage her mind out of the clutches of the sickness that was churning in her stomach.

There was nothing anybody could do about the circumstance they all were caught in. There was absolutely nothing that they could do. Indulging in light conversation was a better way of facing the hell that lay ahead than joining the panic-room of terror and anxiety. It is similar to a doctor trying to make small talk with you to distract you from the imagined fear of the surgery or even just a shot in your arm.

Is distraction a solution to handle fear? Does distraction help in *overcoming* fear? It is understanding that wards off fear. Once you understand, there is nothing to be afraid of. The amount of time and energy that people spend in being afraid, if they could spend that much time and energy in understanding the issue or problem at hand, they would rise above it. A fearless person is also an understanding person.

Sarah needed to understand the transience and the fragility of human existence. What started must end. What lives must die. Why does that make one afraid? If that is the truth then what is there to fear? Fear is an indicator of a lie, of an untruth, of a half-truth. If Sarah could see through the lies and if she knew the truth about her eternity, if she knew the truth about her immortality, she would have nothing to fear.

Jim looked much younger to her. Jim tried hard to focus on her eyes. Their bodies were jolting with the turbulence and his vision was blurring with all the shaking. The plane was about to take the ill-fated plunge into disaster and Jim still found enough peace in the depths of her eyes.

"You don't look nineteen," Sarah nudged Jim.

"Let me see your passport." Sarah was determined not to pay attention to fear and engage instead with a very eager Jim. She plucked out his passport from the seat pocket.

Paul was watching Sarah intensely. He could sense her fear and he could also sense her attempt to distract herself from it, something she had done all her life. Denial and distraction had been her solution to problems she could not solve. Paul could see Jim creating a safe environment for Sarah. Jim, like everyone else, knew something was wrong, majorly wrong, but he was doing the best he could to keep the situation light and uptone for Sarah.

This *is* love, this *is* innocence, this *is* purity, Paul thought.
"Give it back," Jim put his arms around Sarah in an attempt to snatch his passport back. The turbulence, the instability of the flight, did not steal his spirit of indulgence in play.

The passengers at the back were flabbergasted to witness Sarah and Jim's carefree behaviour in an intensely grim situation. Either they were high on drugs or near drunk. They directed their attention to them as a distraction from their own anxiety.
"Give it back," Jim nudged her while Sarah stretched her arm out to Muttu.

"Take it," she squealed as Jim poked a finger in her stomach, tickling her.

Muttu took the passport, not with the intention of participating in their silly flirtatious game, but with the purpose of snapping it open to the front page.

Jimmy Yale. 6th December 1993. The numbers hit Muttu with a potency that could have given him a heart attack.

Jim snapped his seat belt open; he rolled over Sarah and snatched his passport back from a horrified Muttu. Jim had lied. The prediction was false.

Paul saw Muttu's face. Muttu opened his laptop. He deleted the 1 from the 1991 and punched in the number 3. His finger trembled at the 'enter' button and Paul understood why.

"Hit it!" Paul insisted as Muttu sat frozen.

Jim had lied. Muttu's relief had been transient. He was happy that maybe there was an alternate fate as long as someone was going to live. Was he ready to read Jim's future when the vibe had already sent him the reading?

"Hit it," Paul said urgently. He had not made peace with his end. He had wanted to rest in peace and when that window had opened up, he was anything but peaceful.

Sudden screams added to the tension and then the sudden silence worked up the mystery—*is this the end?* The wings of the aircraft were flapping like a bird, threatening to tear loose. The urgency was building up in everybody, the adrenaline spiking their blood stream, a state experienced under extreme stress.

Muttu took one look outside, he held his laptop tight since it was shaking and hitting against the table, as he raised his hand and pressed 'enter.'

Sarah and Jim giggled with pretended oblivion to the destiny that was going to reveal their future.

The numbers swirled with the new data and Paul's vision blurred as though he was in a trance, as all the numbers settled in the box that Paul knew so well.

"He has four hours to live." As soon as Muttu completed his sentence about the unfailing verdict of the stars, the plane jerked as though it had hit into a barrier, like a sudden brake. Deafening screams erupted dramatically and, in the next instant, there was silence.

Muttu held Paul's arm as the plane tilted sideward to a bend of forty-five degrees in one massive jerk. He began to chant hastily as the blood-curdling screams echoed through the body of the aircraft. Whether it was the plane screaming for mercy or it was the people it held, one couldn't tell the difference.

Darkness consumed the aircraft and a blackness settled around it. The electric controls flickered as the seat belt and no-smoking signs began to go on and off. The plane jerked, straightened a bit and then dipped sideward again, going around in circles. It was caught like a fish on the line in the thunderstorm.

The trays and trolleys were smashed onto one side. Cathy remained trapped. The food trolley began to leak its contents out, keeping her in place, immobile. Water gushed out from the loose containers and streamed towards one side of the plane.

Sarah was shaking uncontrollably, Jim holding her tight. Her mouth was open, but she couldn't tell whether the screams she heard were her own or from others. Jim was holding onto her with all his might. He would not let anything happen to her. His whole attention was on Sarah and that made him the least scared person on the plane.

One overhead bin creaked with the weight of the bags that were threatening to break it open. Muttu saw the lid of the overhead bin swell. He saw the lock tear loose as a wave of bags poured onto the passengers below, injuring some of them severely.

*****

Robert saw the flash of lightning a few metres ahead, blinding him. Its force thrust the aircraft upward and turned it into a spin. He clutched the armrest with all his might as he sealed his eyes shut. It would soon be over.

Thunder roared through the aircraft, vibrating on its metal exterior as the force of the lightning kept spinning the aircraft, propelling it upward.

There is silence before death. When one can see the end, one surrenders. The three hundred passengers on board SL502 had surrendered. The only sound that prevailed was the rage of the storm. The victims awaited their fate in silence.

The lights were all out. The radar was blank. The beeping had stopped and all one could hear was the crack of the heavens manifesting in thunderclaps. The darkness was more welcome than the light, for each time the electricity whipped up its streak, the plane either lunged or dipped or spun.

Paul lifted his left hand and placed it on Muttu's arm. He had told him the truth. Muttu was pale yellow. Even nearing his end, he had the courtesy to pull out the sickness bag from the seat and haul his stomach out into it as the airplane spun its sinister round.

The plane jerked into line. A bag came flying back from the seat in front. Muttu covered his face to avoid being hit. The blood on the bag was not Muttu's. Someone in front had been badly hit.

"I'm going to the cockpit," Jim put his hand over Sarah's. She was frozen with fear. He swung open his seat belt. He couldn't just wait to die. He had to do something. *What was the pilot doing? Maybe he needed help. The plane was obviously out of control and the pilot was overwhelmed by the situation. The pilot must be doing his best to salvage the situation. His life was at stake too,* he thought. Jim wasn't thinking about death, he was thinking about life.

As Jim stood up to cross over Sarah, he leaned towards her. In the darkness, he held her shoulder, "Hold on tight. I am going to help the pilot."

Sarah clutched onto Jim's waist tightly.

"No," she wailed. "Don't go. Don't leave me." She pulled him onto her. Jim plopped onto the seat losing his balance and at that exact moment, three mingled rays of greenish blue light ran through the aisle with blinding force and then the thunder hit. The plane lunged upward sixty degrees and then heaved into a fall.

Lightning had struck the nose of the plane repeatedly and

finally made it through from nose to tail. The charge had been seen and felt. The jolt had put into shock the hearts of those whose eyes were open to witness the wrath. The ones with their eyes closed had felt the force like a slap, which brought them back to the reality that death was only a kiss away.

Jim had missed the lightning bolt by a foot. Had he been in its way, he would have been flung to his death.

Jim tried to stand up. The lightning pounded the plane into a dive. Jim flew up hitting the ceiling and then landed on Sarah sideways, banging his head onto the seat behind. Sarah held onto his leg and then his chest tightly. Sarah had saved Jim's life for the moment. One step into the aisle and the rays of lightning would have burnt him alive.

The thundercloud was active like an angry beast. Whether they were going up or down or spinning, no one could tell. Havoc had broken loose among everybody on the plane. The smell of fear and urine was strong in the air. The screams had softened into wails. Murmurs and chants were audible in rhythm. The shock of the electric force had jolted two men who had gone into convulsive fits. Luckily, no lives were lost. The electric current in a lightning strike is powerful enough to stop your heart and cut it into half.

The plane swayed aggressively, as though fighting back even though its controls were fast dying out. With one whiplash of lightning, the thundercloud spat the aircraft upward into the blue sky.

"Did you see that?" Captain Legrand asked his co-pilot. Pilots are used to rare and magical phenomena in the skies and 'did you see that?' is a common question up at thirty thousand feet.

ANOTHER CHANCE. ANOTHER SHOT AT LIFE

Captain Holler's mouth dropped open with shock.

"Did that thundercloud just spit out an Airbus?" Captain Holler punched in the buttons on the control.

The voice crackled in the cockpit.

"We just saw a Skyline Airbus being hauled out of a thundercloud. Its controls must be burnt out. It is lunging upward and gaining altitude," Captain Holler reported to ground control.

The Air Traffic Control was abuzz with as much electric energy as the flight SL502 had been subjected to. The Anti-Terrorism Squad had taken over and a strategy for negotiation was formed and near execution.

The two captains listened in horror when the ground control explained the hijack and that the ATS had taken over.

"This didn't look like hijack," Captain Legrand shook his head. "This looked more like suicide." Holler turned his head to catch the fast disappearing aircraft.

"Why would the hijackers lead the aircraft into the thundercloud if they wanted to negotiate for their lives and the lives of other passengers?" Legrand reasoned.

There was silence in the air and on the ground. Colonel

Jack unsuccessfully tried to sound in control, putting the responsibility on the ATS to figure a recovery of SL502. The plane had been spotted north on the Pacific Ocean, making a sharp and fast rise in altitude.

*****

"We are going to die!" The screams and moans buzzed through the airplane.

"Somebody help! My husband is not breathing. Jack! Jack!" A lady yelled and a few passengers huddled to her seat to help him.

"Oh God! Oh my God!" Sarah began to tremble.

"Call the bloody captain!" one passenger marched to a flight attendant and demanded to speak to the captain. The flight attendant faked a smile, giving a false sense of calm and urging him to sit down and fasten his seat belt. Although the cabin crew is trained in handling emergencies, especially handling irate passengers, nothing had prepared them for this.

"You know you are going to die too?" the passenger urged the flight attendant to take some action.

"What is happening?"

"Are we going to crash?"

"Am I going to die?"
The questions invaded the minds of those who were trying hard not to think about them.

A loose thread of hope was waving in the air. Muttu caught

it and linked others with it. "Ommmm ..." he hummed softly, with the sound of the alphabet 'm' vibrating in his body, cancelling out the electric force that had assaulted his own energy. Muttu hummed 'Om' softly. Each chant vibrated for a good thirty seconds before Muttu followed it up with the next. The vibration consumed his body and his mind, neutralizing it from the trauma that he had just been subject to. As Muttu's mind and body settled in a space of calm, his chants grew louder, vibrating and penetrating through the terror that was exploding in the hearts of every person on the flight.

"Oooooommmmmmm," Muttu intensified his chant. Paul joined in. He held Muttu's arm in support and self-assurance. Muttu did not flinch. He was immersed in his faith, in his space of hope.

The chant was drowning out the cries and wails and sobs. A few people calmed down while the others were still shaking with panic.

Sarah leaned towards Muttu. She closed her eyes and tuned into the energy that Muttu was emanating.

The energy penetrated through Sarah and Jim was pulled in. He held Sarah's hand instinctively and the calm consumed him. He joined in the chant.

Hands pulled out, leaving the security of the armrest and reached out for another hand, another soul, whose destiny depended upon the collective fate and karma of all those who were aboard the Flight SL502. Prayers to multiple gods emanated through the aircraft, sending a message of hope to whoever it was that kept hope alive so people could have a chance at alternate destinies.

*****

Paul knew that the word Om when chanted held mystic value for the Hindus in India. Hinduism was a philosophy that was fast penetrating the West.

Paul had indulged in Hinduism in his quest for an answer to 'what have I missed in living, since achievement doesn't make me feel alive anymore'. He knew that, in the Hindu sects, Om is set forth as an object of profound religious meditation. It is the highest spiritual efficacy being attributed to the one word, the one chant, Om. According to the Hindu scriptures, whoever knows this one syllable and chants it in its correct resonance, obtains all he desires. It is also believed that one who departs, leaving the body at death while chanting the word Om, attains the Supreme Goal—salvation.

The aircraft vibrated with the chant, the aircraft vibrated with hope. The chanting had gained support. In the end, people will participate in anything that brings hope of their survival.

Flight SL502 was overwhelmed by the energy of the chant that evoked the gods, bringing their attention to a task that had probably been an oversight. After taking a beating from the thundercloud, SL502 was comforted in the energy of the divine.

*****

The plane was steady now. Minutes had passed and no turbulence had disturbed the state of peace that prevailed in the hearts of the passengers.

The electric controls were still dead, but hope had found a new abode.

Cathy had been stuck for a while now. As soon as she could

reach there, Glenda rushed to her rescue. She tried her best to move the trolley. The lock was jammed, keeping Cathy trapped at the door. Each time she yanked at it, the metal hit Cathy. She bent over and tried to pull the trolley from the wheels and it moved an inch.

"Push!" Glenda instructed, as she pulled at the wheel with all her might. It took the collective strength of both to pull the trolley free of its hold. It took time for Cathy to stand up straight on her feet. She was still shaking from her ordeal.

"Captain Joe," she whispered. The close call with death had not thrown her off her purpose. Purpose is a primary dictator of intention and action. Those who have defined their purpose have also defied every obstacle that stands in their way. Purpose fuels action. No matter how deep the chasm, no matter how high the mountain, when passion is the driving source, the gap is covered and the length is mapped.

Cathy pushed Glenda aside and headed towards the resting cabin. She twisted the knob and pushed, but the door did not budge. She yanked the handle a few times, but the lock stayed in place. The lock was jammed. Cathy looked at Glenda.

"Maybe Captain Joe locked it from inside," Glenda was as confused as Cathy was.

"No, this door doesn't have a lock. Something was off about him as was about Tom." Cathy tried to make sense connecting the two captains. She tried to heave the door, kicking it a few times but the door didn't budge an inch.

"Maybe it was the turbulence and the incline," Glenda reasoned further. Cathy looked at her, narrowing her brows. That seemed to fit. The incline sometimes sets the system off its control, unlocking and locking the latches.

"Is he dead?" Glenda held on to the wall.

"I think so," Cathy said nervously. She felt faint. This was not a hijack. This was murder, suicide, insanity.

*****

Tom had stopped breathing. He stayed motionless on his chair. The cornea of his left eye was split and the blood had streaked into the white of his eye. His skin was turning a deep shade of bluish green. The stroke of lightning only added to the speed of the poison, stopping his heart with the energy as it struck.

Robert sat on his seat bent over in a fetal position. The plane was steady now and maybe this is how death felt. Robert had been in the way of the lightning and it had missed him by a couple of feet when it had struck.

The controls were damaged. The radar was blank. There were no beeps, no sounds and no signals. The electric control was messed up. There was a smell of rubber burning, but that was probably wire burnt in the lightning strike.

Robert opened his eyes. The sunlight stung his eyes after the prolonged bout of darkness and hell. The sky was blue and the sun was shining sleepily, getting up on its rise. What had he done? He had brought poison to kill himself and his co-pilot was dead. He had flown the aircraft into the thundercloud as a suicide attempt and he had still made it through. Was it not his time to die? Or was someone's karma holding his evil intentions at bay?

An uncanny calm prevailed in the aircraft. Tom was dead and

looked ghastly. The poison and then the lightning had done a dirty job of killing him. By now, his door should have been pounded down by the flight attendants and the passengers. Why wasn't anyone reacting? Robert shifted uneasily in his seat.

What should I do now? The question resounded in his head. Surprisingly, Robert felt regret. Was what he was doing fair? Were his actions justified? His life was miserable. But the people who left him didn't intend that. His friends had died serving their purpose as he was serving his. It is incidental that they died and he didn't. If he had died in the collision instead of his buddy, would it have been his friend's fault? Why was he then blaming himself? He had died as a matter of circumstance. When one signs up for the air force, one makes peace with his own death and those of others. Robert looked around, trying to avoid looking at Tom's body.

What was happening to him? Why were these thoughts aligning logically in his head? Rationale and reason had been missing from his emotional response for many years now. How come this sudden surge of realization?

His family had died in a car crash. Was it their fault that they had died? They were headed to attend a wedding. The bride and groom attended their funeral instead. It was a drunk, irresponsible driver. He had not only killed Robert's family, but had sentenced him to a life of heartache and despair. As much as he wanted to end his life and not wake up to another day of misery, would killing three hundred families be a solution to his pain?

The end brings with it the unfolding of the truth. Many say that they will be held accountable at the pearly gates of Heaven. The preparation for that account seems to start with the first hint of death. The truth comes to fore and one can see through the falsities, the unnecessary lies, the unimportant games and the absolutely useless defenses. And then life begins to make sense, in the end.

Robert rubbed his face nervously. Why were these thoughts infesting his mind? What should he do now?

If he landed the plane safely, he would be locked up in prison for the rest of his life.

"Do I want that?" Robert muttered. Living in prison would be worse than dying now.

Maybe, he thought, if he did some damage control and said that Tom was trying to poison him and that he'd accidently swapped the coffee and then Tom drank it, becoming a victim to his own plan, maybe that would work as a story, saving him, the three hundred people aboard, and the three hundred families that waited for them on ground.

But how would that explain cutting off the radio and not responding to the flight attendants? Maybe he could say that Tom fought with him and that Tom was threatening to crash the aircraft. That would seem like a plausible story.

He could salvage the situation. He could find a way to get out of this. It was sad that Tom had to die, but three hundred others need not share the same fate. *He* didn't want to. After all the planning and scheming, he didn't want to die anymore. He had been to the gates of death and back, and life seemed more palatable now. How does one really want to know that one wants to die until one experiences or touches what death is? Robert had touched that line and he didn't want it. He just needed a plan that would keep him clear of a hell, which awaited him on the ground, should he survive.

He had half a day to perfect his plan, to create a perfect lie. And that is how his life would be going forward, in a cover-up. Little did he know that he would spend the rest of his days not really living; he would spend the rest of his days covering up the truth he had missed living up to.

"Ladies and gentlemen, this is your captain speaking. We had an unfortunate situation and I apologize to you for that. The situation is now under control. Stay calm. We are going home."

Robert could imagine the relief of the passengers on board. He was right. Every passenger was heaving a sigh of relief at the announcement. The sense of relief was so immense that the whole plane would have caught some speed with the collective release of wind from three hundred bodies.

Robert put his hands on the controls. None of them seemed to be working. He tried turning the aircraft, the controls were dead. He tried to push the throttle to increase the speed, it was dead. He tried to drop altitude, he tried to raise it—no change. Robert had seen the lightning passing through the aircraft. That meant that it must have struck the nose more than once. The nose of the aircraft is fitted with lightning resistant strips just for this reason. If lightning strikes the controls, the plane is dead.

With trembling hands, Robert flipped on the radio. Every word he uttered here onward could and would be used against him.

He had decided to do the right thing the wrong way, yet again.

"SL502 making contact," he said nervously and waited for a response. There was none. All electric connections were dead.

*****

Applause echoed through the aircraft. There were blessings and expressions of gratitude to a hundred different gods. Not many are given a second chance. For some like Glenda, it had been the umpteenth. With her, the fear and integrity didn't last long. When things and life were back to normal, she was back to her irresponsible ways.

Sarah and Jim hugged tight. "I told you everything would be all right," Jim took credit for the situation. He had held his fort of courage and bravery, and the situation had eventually turned out fine, like he had said it would.

Paul let out a sigh of relief, as did Muttu. They looked at each other nervously. They had been through an extremely vulnerable moment. Two men, equally successful, equally spiritual, sharing the same views about life and death, going through the same experience. Was this a coincidence, or was it meant to be?

A few passengers got up and thanked Muttu. They could trace the change of fate to the energy from his chanting. What they had been through was a sheer miracle.

Muttu was embarrassed with all the attention. He didn't want to take any credit for the situation, since that would only put more responsibility on him in the future. He had only done what he knew best—to surrender.

"Your vibe, your chanting had a positive effect, Muttu. The source of this miracle is you," Paul held Muttu's arm and Muttu only squirmed with that compliment.

"With you here, our future is safe," Paul looked out of the window. The skies were exceptionally calm. There was no sight or trace of the thunderclouds or their like. The skies were open with an aura of unmistakable divinity.

"Why don't you look up your own future, Muttu?" Paul posed the question that no one had dared to bring up in Muttu's career.

"I cannot," Muttu shook his head.

"Why not?" Paul asked. Why couldn't Muttu look up his own destiny? It didn't make sense.

"Because I don't want to be self-absorbed. Isn't that what everyone is doing? People are so consumed with their own survival and problems that they have stopped living. They are so submerged in their insecurities that they come to me. If I see my future, I will become one of them. Let my life unfold what it holds for me. I am handling my present with grace, humility and sincerity. I am doing the right thing to the best of my ability and knowledge. My future is a response to who I am and what I do today. I don't care about what lies in store for me tomorrow. I am living today in the service of others. My profession has no service for me," Muttu explained.

"But you see our destinies are intertwined. I am going to die in," Paul looked at his watch, "in three hours. Sarah and Jim are going to die in three hours as well. Don't you want to know the end and then embrace it, if that is the only future your destiny holds? How will you know if you should surrender, or fight for your survival?" Paul's voice shook.

Muttu was lost in thought. His end was near, but did he want his computer to prove it to him? Would that knowledge serve him? What would he do if the stars showed that he, like the rest of the passengers in the row, had only three hours to live? Would that change the way he would live in the next three hours?

Muttu opened his laptop. He punched in his date of birth. Paul was six years younger to him. At fifty-two, life had served him well. The numbers were ready and Muttu's hand trembled at 'enter.'

Paul allowed him his time. You can't push people to see their future.

Muttu's index finger rested on 'enter'. A little more pressure would send the numbers flying to consult with the stars and align. Muttu did not need a laptop to know where the numbers would sway. He did not need the stars to tell him which box held his fate. He did not need to know. *He knew.*

Muttu slammed the laptop shut.

*****

Glenda had been on the phone with the other flight attendants in business and economy; her worry and hopelessness had grown with every call. Glenda picked up the receiver, but before she could punch in the cockpit code, Cathy caught her hand and put the receiver back on its rack.

"Don't question goodness," she said, placing a hand on Glenda's shoulder.

She headed to the resting cabin and tried the door again. It was locked.

"Where is Paul?" Glenda's attention finally went back to her dream-date passenger. All was well and it took a few minutes for her to spring back to her usual self. "Should I page for him?" she asked Cathy. Cathy seemed the more sensible between the two and Glenda was allowing her to make the decisions.

"Let me check with the flight attendants in economy," Cathy got on the phone and signalled a thumbs-up to Glenda. Paul was in economy, seated on 26F with no hurry or intention to get back to the zone where he belonged.

Glenda walked to the resting cabin. Captain Joe had to be either dead or unconscious. There was no effort on his part to get out. He couldn't be in such deep sleep as to not have been woken up with the thundercloud episode. But what if he was alive?

Glenda plucked out her hairpin. She was good with locks. It was in her nature to get her way, regardless of whether others liked it or not. She stuck the hairpin into the gap between the door and the latch. She twisted it. It was jammed. It wasn't locked. It was jammed. She tried a few more times, but the latch stayed in place. Her hairpin twisted and a frustrated Glenda went back to her seat.

*****

Muttu kept staring at the blank TV screen ahead. Paul allowed him his space. That is the greatest respect one can give to another—the privacy of his space, the time of his silence. Something had shifted in his vibe. He looked like a man who was ready—ready for any future that lay ahead of him.

Muttu turned about and looked at Sarah. Her eyes were tightly shut, all attention directed inwards. Something was going on in her mind and it was not Mike. She was thinking about her book, her purpose. She loved to write and she had quit, based on what someone else thought.

Would one abandon one's child if someone else did not approve of him? Would one give up what one loves if someone else didn't love it? Sarah's mind was alive with her purpose. Why had she subjected her dreams to someone else's approval? How stupid had she been! It took an astrologer on a flight to tell her that her dream was alive, and she was the one who was killing it.

Muttu tapped Sarah's shoulder and her blood-red eyes shot open. Tears poured out of her eyes as she took a long sob.

"I will write the last chapter," she said. "Thank you."

Muttu was startled by his act of reaching out to her, for he felt that he owed Sarah his time. He knew she didn't have much time left and he could make the hours longer by putting some of his energy into her life.

"I can look into the future," he said to Sarah.

"The numbers show me the time that lies ahead. I have spent all of my life showing others what they feared most—their future. Sometimes I held the bad news back and sometimes, I put more hope than was apparent. My second granddaughter was born seven days ago. She will grow up to be a healer. She has a special gift. She can perceive energy and shift it. The world will be a beneficiary of her presence. My son has trying times ahead and will move back to India. It will be for the better. I didn't tell him that because he is not ready to see the future. He has denied acceptance of the present. My daughter suffers because she creates negative realities in her mind. If all reality is first created in the mind, then why not create a positive one? Why complain about the state of the world? If we could just take responsibility for the state of our minds, wouldn't the world reflect that? My wife is nearing her time. I don't want to see when. She is the woman I admire most and the only woman that I have ever loved. She looks after me to the point where I wouldn't know what to do with myself if she left me. I always prayed that I should go before her. She is much stronger than I am," Muttu paused gathering himself and Sarah allowed him his space, holding his hand. Tears began to well up in her eyes, but she repressed her sobs. This was not about her; she had to allow him to unburden his heart. She held on to Muttu's hand.

"My life has been all about numbers—seven has been my luckiest number, the most auspicious one according to my birth chart. Coincidentally, the flight I got on was SL502. Nothing evil or negative can come to me as long as seven is my number. I have faith in that, I have faith in that knowing, I have faith in the belief that I have lived my whole life by. How can death then be negative or evil?" Sarah's eyes were glued onto Muttu's. She was listening to him intently. His Indian accent was no longer a deterrent, she understood him completely.

"My numbers show that my future is safe, like is everyone else's. It depends how far a future you can see. I saw a future—my future—beyond the mortality of the body, beyond this lifetime, and it is safe. When the body dies, I will move into the future and build another one, or not."

A few more rows in the front and the back were also tuned into Muttu's narration. They had been through hell and back together and the journey back to peace seemed to have sprung from Row 26. Every now and then, the attention shifted to the row from where divinity seemed to be emanating.

"What does my destiny hold?" Muttu turned to Paul, who needed no permission to participate in the conversation. He was already leaning in, involved.

"I remember a story one of my Gurus told me," Muttu choked, as all ears were alert in his direction.

"He is telling a story from his Guru," whispered some of the passengers.

"Shhh," shushed some other passengers as they tried to hear the story.

"There was a small village in India near Rajasthan. On the footsteps of the village temple sat a middle-aged man called Gopi. He was dressed in ragged clothes, like one who has lost all interest in life. No one had seen him before; he seemed to have appeared at the temple overnight. He didn't look like a beggar for he never troubled anyone who came to the temple. He did not ask for alms. He just sat there gazing at nothing in particular.

"Days passed by. Some said he was waiting for something to happen; others said he was waiting for someone to arrive. There were rumors about the motive of his presence.

"'What are you doing here?' the head priest of the village eventually asked him.

"'I am waiting for my time to come,' he replied, firm on a purpose that no one understood.

"'He is waiting to die,' some hushed. Others thought he was a learned man who was waiting for his time, or the god who kept time to emerge.

"'I will summon the God of Time for you. Your time will come,' the priest promised and returned to the temple. He evoked the god that kept time, to answer this man's strange entreaty.

"Come dawn, the God of Time made his appearance duly, at the request of the head priest.

"'I have come,' The lord announced his presence. 'What is it you want?' He demanded of Gopi.

"'I have been waiting for you to take me,' the man bowed his head, requesting an end to his life-term.

"The whole village gasped at this request. With the hundreds of rituals that they performed for good health and a long life, here was a man that was praying for just the opposite.

"'Okay. I will grant you the death you desire. With your karma, the fastest that I can take you is in three months.' the God of Time complied.

"'Three months?!' Gopi protested. It was apparently too much for him.

"'That's how long it would take for you to die of liver and kidney failure if I started your clock now,' the Lord reasoned.
"Gopi thought about it. He could see the three months of pain and illness. He could see the physical and mental turmoil that would follow as a result of his organ failures. He could see the spiritual challenge in surviving the disillusion that this painful manner of death would bring everyday. It was not about dying after three months, it was about dying every day for three months.

"'Give me a better option, O Lord of Time. Something soon.

Very soon,' the man begged. 'It is better to die for a purpose than at the mercy of circumstance. Give me a purpose that I can die for.'

"'I have a pick-up for six people tomorrow night, in the third village from here. It's a group who will attempt to redirect the river Saraswati towards their village. They will risk and eventually give up their lives to fulfil their purpose of bringing water to their village, so that their fellow men can live. If you can swap places with one of them, then you can be a part of the group that I am scheduled to pick up.' With those words, the Lord disappeared as mystically as he had appeared.

"It was for the first time that people saw joy on the man's face. He was delighted that his time had come. He was ready to head for the third village and put his life to a purposeful end. As a parting gift to a man who was on his way to the other world, the villagers gave him a horse so he could make it in time to the third village to end his term for this lifetime.

"Gopi rode all through the night tirelessly and arrived at dawn at the third village. An aura of death loomed over the village. It looked like it had no inhabitants. The ground was dry and cracked open. There was no sign of life or vegetation. Dried trees lay fallen at intervals. The skeleton of a cow by the village square added to the spookiness of the area. Gopi rode on through the deserted streets. He then heard the sound of beating drums and turned his horse in that direction.

"A fire was emanating thick black smoke while a small group of villagers drummed furiously. It was a mix of men, women and some children. They were praying hard to the Rain God and the God of the Rivers to send them water.

"Gopi watched as six men stepped forward as volunteers.

"'Bring us Saraswati. Save our lives,' the villagers began to adorn them with streaks of coloured ash and prayer threads. These were the men who were going to pass by the land of the Mighty Snake and redirect the Saraswati River so that the village and its remaining lives could be saved.

"'I will go,' Gopi interrupted the startled villagers.

"'My time has come. I will go,' he proclaimed.

"One young lady rushed forward and pulled her husband back from the line-up.

"The villagers took one look at Gopi and shouted in unison, 'Let there be water!'

"The five men, along with Gopi, galloped towards the hills, leaving behind them a dust cloud. When it settled, the men were gone.

"The river Saraswati held in it enough water to supply the entire country for a hundred years, let alone the third village. A canal was already built by the villagers, which would bring in the abundant supply of water, but the Mighty Snake was blocking the route to that passage. All one had to do was destroy the block to the river and there would be water.

"The Mighty Snake was the King Cobra, the seven-headed serpent blessed by the gods with immortality as long as it stayed away from water. The purposes of the Mighty Snake and the villagers were in conflict, where each was bound to its survival.

"The Mighty Snake had already sensed the arrival of the six men and waited for them at the boundary of his land, the

Saraswati dancing a mile away in the distance.

"'You have come again?' the Mighty Snake bellowed, with the eyes of his seven heads spitting fire. 'Turn around before I burn you to ashes like your predecessors.' The fifty-foot long serpent raised his seven heads off the ground, towering over the horsemen.

"Five of them pulled the reigns to their horses and stopped in their tracks. Gopi however trotted on.

"'Stop, before I evaporate your existence,' the Mighty Snake threatened, announcing to Gopi that his time had indeed come. Gopi smiled at the perplexed Mighty One. This man was not scared of him? This man was not afraid to die? Who was he?

"'Stop!' the Mighty Snake hissed another warning, as he fanned out his hood over a few metres.

"'O Mighty Snake! O Immortal One! The third village has been dying. They have no water. There are only a few left before their existence is wiped off too. They need the water,' Gopi put forward his reason for being there, while the five horsemen waited for the final verdict.

"'If I release the water, I will die,' the Mighty Snake fanned out closer to the ground to get a good look at this small and frail man, who had the courage to keep inching closer to him.

"'And if you don't, they will die, O Mighty One,' Gopi reasoned back.

"'If someone must die, let it be them,' the Mighty Snake lunged back hovering over Gopi.

"'They have died already. Many of them. Most of them. A few more weeks and the third village will cease to exist. And then the same fate will befall the fourth village and then the fifth. They need the water,' Gopi's voice turned soft. He was standing up for people he had never met. He was speaking for the people who had lost their lives in the pain he did not want to experience. Many had not had a chance for a dignified death or even a dignified life. He didn't need to know them to understand them and to feel their misery. The ones left wanted to live. They wanted water.

"'Let there be water, O Mighty One. Let them live,' Gopi folded his hands.

"'Why should I die?' the Mighty Snake snorted.

"'Because life isn't to be protected. Life is to be lived. What will you do with immortality, if your life doesn't serve a purpose? What will you do with your life everyday if every day marks the end of several lives because you live? You have lived already, for thousands of years. You have seen all there is to be seen. You have heard all there is to be heard. You know more than they do. Immortality is a boon when granted for a purpose, but a curse when it ceases to be one,' Gopi choked over his own words.
"'Why should I care about their lives?' the Mighty One bowed, extending his tail in Gopi's direction.

"Gopi dismounted his horse and stepped on his tail and with one swoop the Mighty Snake lifted him above the ground and brought him face-to-face with his seven heads.

"'You should care because that's who you are. You don't need to know people to extend life to them, to extend love to them. You do that because that's who you are—you emanate it. The sun doesn't choose who benefits from its sunlight. The sun shines because that's what it is; it can't help but spread out its warmth. Who heals from it is incidental, it is not a part of its purpose, it's a part of the sun's being.

"'Why should I care? Has anyone ever cared about me?' the Mighty Snake's heads drooped. It had been granted the boon of immortality but, without love, immortality is a curse. The quality of one's life is not determined by its length. Even a few moments of love measure larger than an eternity without it.

"'No one ever cared for me,' the Mighty Snake hissed with remorse. He had lived a life in isolation. Everyone feared him. No one neared him. And when someone did, they never returned home.

"'I do,' Gopi stretched his hand out to the Mighty One. 'I do,' he repeated.

"The Mighty Snake constricted his fan as the seven heads closed into one. His eyes narrowed as he pulled his tail closer to his eyes. Gopi stood close to his face, swaying with every breath that the Mighty Snake took.

"'I will go with you,' Gopi touched his nose, as the Mighty Snake extended his tongue in a sudden hiss.

"'I will go with you,' Gopi repeated. 'If you can give your life for others, then I can give my life for you. I am not asking you to give up your life. I am asking you to save the lives of a thousand others. I am willing to go with you on the journey that waits ahead of this bondage. Immortality is not what you need, freedom is what your soul awaits. Let's go. Let them live till they find out for themselves, that saving their life is the most distracting of all purposes. Let's live. Let's live beyond the need for water, beyond the need for sunshine, beyond the need for food. Let's live for the sake of love, for freedom.'

"The Mighty One closed his eyes and bowed his head. One large ball of tear rolled down and splashed on the parched ground. The drops burned into the skin of the Mighty Snake and it twitched with the pain. One more tear built up and Gopi cupped his hands to catch it and save him the pain.

"'Give them the water,' he hissed as a large wave of tears welled up in his eyes.

"'Give them the water!!' Gopi yelled as the five men charged at the Saraswati, releasing the blocks to the canal.

"A large tsunami wave of excitement built in the river as Saraswati was allowed to fulfill her purpose—to create life. As the water roared free, it swallowed the five horsemen into its depths and then churned them out into the sea fulfilling their appointment with the God of Time.

"A stream of tears poured out of the eyes of the Mighty Snake as Gopi held tightly onto his head, his face inches away from his right eye.

"'Thank you,' he kissed his head.

"'Thank you for helping me realize that life without a purpose is death. I was waiting to die for life had no purpose for me. That is death. I was waiting. You helped me realize that purpose is life; death is only a temporary consequence of the body. I am not dying today. I am free. And I am going with you.'

"The Mighty Snake coiled his tail around Gopi in an attempt to protect him from the hell that would break loose seconds later. When the wave crashed on them, it was over in seconds. The immortal Mighty Snake and Gopi merged into the river Saraswati, for all eternity."

The blood in Muttu's arm had stopped flowing for Sarah had clutched it so tightly. A streak of tears burned down her cheeks. These were not tears of fear, these were tears of purpose, tears of freedom.

Paul stared at Muttu expressionless.

"You knew you were going to die when you took this flight," he mumbled inaudibly. "You knew we all were going to die, right?" he whispered.

Paul saw the truth in Muttu's eyes. He had heard it in his voice. He had got the message from his story.

"Yes," Muttu looked at him intensely. "But I hoped, for the first time, that what I saw would be untrue, that there lay an alternate future for me and for everyone else. It made me nervous. I had left everything behind. I had wound up all the loose ends. But then there is an urge to hold on to that which is destined to end, and not to let go. I hoped beyond hope that I was wrong. I turned to Sarah but the future ahead stayed set—unchanging. How the end unfolds is a matter of circumstance. That it will unfold as I see it is a certainty," Muttu paused. "But" his voice turned soft, "I can see a new beginning after it all ends. But, I am still instinctively bound not to let go!"

"I will go with you," Muttu looked towards Paul. He had the urge to tell Sarah and Jim the truth, but he didn't feel the need to disturb their state of hope. They didn't need to know. They were not ready.

"You are a good man. Your life and your purpose have served many. I will go with you. Not because I am destined to, but because I choose to."

*****

Colonel Jack was sipping his seventh coffee.

"Yes, over the Pacific, 180 degrees latitude," he gave instructions to the ATS in-charge. "The radio is still out and we have no radar visibility. The Airbus could be anywhere now. We need to act fast."

The E-9A Widget was deployed to keep track of flight SL502, and to initiate radio contact for negotiation. Two trained Anti-Terrorism generals were aboard the flight tearing through the sky towards the Pacific Ocean.

The entire passenger list was sitting on Jack's desk and the names were already being screened for criminal histories. The information was withheld from the media and would become public only if the flight did not land in New York.

The E-9A Widget is one of the fastest fighter planes of the US Military. When a pilot says the word 'help', the ATS takes that very seriously. The Widget would be tailing the flight, so its location could be sent back to ATC. It would connect to the ground to ensure that all negotiation could be handled, to save the lives of the three hundred passengers on board.

*****

Robert was staring at the sky ahead. He had no idea what altitude the plane was flying at. He would estimate thirty-five thousand feet plus. What confused him was why the plane was still ascending? Why was it still rising?

The lightning had thrown the plane upward and it was on a very slow and sinister ascent. Luckily, for the three hundred passengers, the controls were jammed on the ascent; if the controls had jammed on a descent, the aircraft would fall to the ground within minutes. He needed the controls back fast. Robert kept fidgeting with the controls in the hope that the circuit would fall in place. Lightning has that effect on electronics. How long they would be down, no one could tell.

Robert's immediate concern was his story, which would ensure his survival. He had been in the air force long enough to know the reprimand drill. He knew the questions, the areas that would raise suspicion and so he began to work his way through them. If anything went wrong, then suicide was his plan anyway.

Robert was aggressively flipping the controls. It was the voice on the radio that threw him back in his chair. When you have a dead man inches away from you, any human sound can give you a heart attack.

"SL502, come in. Do you copy?" the voice crackled.

Robert was stunned. He wasn't expecting the radio to go on. The radar was still blank. Did he imagine the sound?

Robert remained silent.

"SL502, come in. Do you copy?" the voice crackled urgently again.

✳✳✳✳✳

"What do you mean, Muttu?" Paul looked at him confused. Muttu had not pressed 'enter.' He had never read his own chart. What was he talking about? How could he say that he was going to die?

"I was born with a gift," Muttu said gravely. "I could tell the future. I could look at a person, hear a person's voice, just hear the mention of an event and I would know. It was as though I was tuned in to everyone and everything. My abilities began to spook my friends and they no longer wanted to be friends with me. When I was five, I predicted my grandfather's death and my relatives shunned me as evil. Later, when my grandfather did die as I had seen it, they said it was my evil eye. I learnt early to keep quiet—to know and to not tell.

"As I grew up, I learnt that my ability, my gift, had a use. If I could tell you there was trouble ahead, that did not ward off the trouble but it prepared you for it. A prepared person is better off than an unprepared person. I learnt that if I could tell you what lay ahead, then you could make the necessary changes needed to face it better.

"So I took the aid of my computer and numbers. I don't need them. I use them so I can stay human. With the predictions that I make, if anyone knew *I* made them, I would be given the position of demi-god. I am no god. I am like you and everyone else—the only difference is that I have retained my powers and you have forgotten.

"I don't need my laptop to know my destiny. I know. However, as much as I know, and I have known it since I was four years old, I must confess my purpose is not yet complete. And so, for the first time, I wanted a way out, to verify, if for once I could be wrong," Muttu smiled.

Paul was stunned. He had hoped that Muttu was wrong, and he had not believed him when he had said that his end was near.

"Are we all going to die?" Paul asked him hesitatingly.

"At this point, I don't need my abilities. I need my purpose so I can plan my departure to step into the future that awaits me," Muttu looked grave, avoiding Paul's question. He was already dealing with a truth that was too heavy for him and Muttu did not want to increase his burden.

*****

Glenda and Cathy had had it easy being in first class. The flight attendants in the economy section were on their toes handling passengers, for they seemed to be beeping for them every five seconds.

"Should I buzz the cockpit?" Glenda asked. She wanted to see Captain Robert for herself to be assured that everything was all right.

"He could be hungry," Glenda reasoned.

"Then he will call. Something has changed. The captain was behaving weird. Tom was acting weird too. Something had happened, something awful. But," Cathy pressed Glenda's hand, "something has changed now. Don't disturb it. Let it flow. If Robert needs us, he will buzz. Did he not buzz the passengers?"

Glenda agreed that the behaviour of all the three captains was disconcerting and took Cathy's advice to leave it alone.

*****

The beep on the radar brought some life back into the cockpit. The plane was at thirty-nine thousand feet and still climbing. Robert began to yank at the controls and felt some vibration come on. It couldn't be from the aircraft, it had to be from another machine in the vicinity.

Robert looked out the window, and the skies were clear. There was no aircraft in sight. He ticked the controls on and off, and the lights came on. He breathed a sigh of relief. He turned the altitude down, bringing the notches to settle at thirty thousand feet.

"SL502. Do you copy?" the radio crackled again.

Robert closed his eyes and took a deep breath, "Captain Robert from SL502. I copy."

"Contact made!" Colonel Jack yelled in the control room, as Robert's voice came in from the radio of the Widget.

"Lieutenant General Sanders from the ATS. We are ready to negotiate. Do you copy?" the voice came in.

Robert's heart stopped beating at that transmission. The vibration that was still felt was not from the Airbus, it was from the Widget in the vicinity. They had traced him. They were at his tail. He had to think quickly. He knew the implications of this matter.

"Damn !!!" he pounded on the armrest.

"Captain Tom was trying to hijack the plane. He tried to poison Joe and me. Joe is probably dead. Tom accidentally consumed the poison he was trying to kill me with. Gave me a fight. Took the plane into a thundercloud and attempted to take us all down." Robert said his well-rehearsed speech.

"Where is Tom now?" Lieutenant General Sanders asked.

"He is dead. The poison and the lightning got him," Robert said. The only hitch in speaking on the radio is that you cannot evaluate the other person's response. It cuts out the communication until the radio comes on again.

"Any terrorists? Any hostages? Any casualties?" Sanders shot the questions.

"Negative for all," Robert was getting in form now, more alert, more cooperative.

"We are ready for a negotiation, Captain," Sanders waited for an answer, as did ATC.

"Negative Captain. The assassin is dead," Robert reassured.

"What's the position now? What's the damage?" the Lieutenant General asked urgently. Robert's explanation was not close to satisfactory, but, at the moment, he wanted to get the plane safely on land.

"The controls are coming back now," Robert saw the lights come up slowly on the buttons.

"Prepare to land, Captain. I am clearing the New Guinea airbase for you," Lieutenant General Sanders ordered.

"Bringing SL502 in at the New Guinea airbase. Bring in the Squad." Sanders barked in the orders to ATC.

"Well done," Jack congratulated Sanders for his quick and efficient resolution.

"I wouldn't count on it. The assassin is still alive," Sanders assured ground control.

THE CONQUEST OF FEAR

"Are you afraid? Do you feel fear?" Paul tried to borrow Muttu's calm. He wanted to know what he was feeling because his posture was much calmer than his.

"When you boarded the flight, you knew you were going to die; why, then, would you take the flight? Why didn't you stay home?" Paul couldn't understand Muttu.

"Ask.com reveals that 1,46,357 people die each day in the world. That makes it 6,098 people dying every hour. Do you think my geographical location will impact my fate? I will die wherever I am if it is my time to go. It doesn't matter whether I am on a flight, or in a car, or at home," Muttu spoke with a calm not befitting a man who knew he was about to die in the next two hours.

"Didn't you want to spend the time with your family?" Paul was curious.

"My wife dropped me at the airport. Her journey with me ended there. She was happy. I was happy. We bade each other goodbye. How else would I want to leave her?"

"My son booked my ticket. He chose the date of my flight. I checked the numbers—they were mine—numbers that brought me the greatest luck."

"Wouldn't he blame himself for your death?" Paul was alarmed. If he had booked his father's ticket on a plane that never landed, he would never make peace with himself.

"I know I am going to die. Who must I blame for it? My son is an evolved soul; he will see the truth for himself. When it is his time to go, no matter what anyone does or does not do, it will end for him when his time is up. If one has to blame oneself, one will do it irrespective of the circumstances. Blame doesn't need permission of the person in question. Blame is an indicator of one's own regret, of a life unlived, of people unloved, of time wasted. Blame is not real, it's always imaginary.

"Even if a person dies an ordinary death, their loved ones will still blame themselves for his passing. 'I should have done this. I should have done that. I shouldn't have done this. I shouldn't have done that.' Regret and blame are close friends. Where you find one, you also find the other.

"My son is an evolved soul. He won't play the blame game."

"Four people dying … all at the same time. Will there be more?" Paul asked, biting his lip.

"1,46,357 for the day," Muttu smiled.

"Out of 1,46,357, will there be three hundred from this flight?" Paul asked nervously.

*****

The phone in the service galley buzzed. Glenda made a dash for it.

"Prepare the cabin for landing. We will be cutting our trip short at New Guinea. We will need a change of aircraft," Robert spoke, to Glenda's relief.

"Oh thank you, Captain," she was on the verge of tears. "How long to destination?"

"Approximately two hours," Robert estimated.

"Can I bring you something to eat? Are you all right, Captain?" Glenda sounded concerned.

"Is Captain Tom okay? We think Captain Joe is unconscious, or— " she stopped before using the word dead. "His cabin is locked and we are unable to open it. He hasn't tried to break free either," Glenda began to blurt incessantly.

Robert listened to her story and her despair. He could use Glenda as an ally. He could fill her in with the details of his story and then use her as a witness. Robert knew Glenda to be a scatterbrain and somewhat of a loose character. He could manipulate her.

"Tom tried to poison me. He assaulted me and then drove the aircraft into the thunderstorm. As fate would have it, he accidentally consumed his own poison," Robert told the same story he had told the Chief General of the ATS.

"Tom is dead?" Glenda was aghast. Cathy had been right all this time.

"This is such a relief. I am sure you will be a hero when the world finds out that you saved the lives of three hundred passengers. ATC has all the radio recordings. I am sure they already know about your heroic deed. Thank you, Captain, for saving our lives. Can I bring you some water? Something to eat?" Glenda asked. There was silence.

"Hello, Captain!" Glenda was alarmed. "Hello?" She waited for a response. With a click, the line went dead.

Glenda looked around confused. *What happened? What had happened now?*

She walked up to the cockpit door and knocked.

"Captain! Are you all right?" She punched in the code, the door remained locked.

*****

"The assassin is on board," the Colonel chewed on his cigarette.

"Why doesn't he want to negotiate?" he asked the Chief of the ATS, who had just heard on the radio, the conversation between Robert and Sanders, and who had also received the recording from the cockpit radio minutes later.

"He is a psycho. He wants to kill. That is his only motive," the Chief of the ATS declared.

"Robert says Tom tried to poison him. Whereas Robert was the one who had spiked the coffee with the Vitamin C, or the poison. Tom was normal; Robert was the one who was behaving weird. The coffee had the poison, which Robert had put in it," The Chief of the ATS explained. "Whether it was an attempt at suicide or a plan for mass murder, we will find out when we have Robert in custody."

"Lie low on your contact with SL502; let us bring the three hundred passengers to safety first. The Anti-Terrorism Squad is ready to receive them."

Jack stared thoughtfully out of the window. From Major to Pilot to Terrorist. This was a long spiral downward for Robert. He had known Robert since his air force days. He was intelligent, committed and determined. It was only after he lost his family that he had started breaking down. He withdrew from friends and colleagues, and kept pretty much to himself.

Dealing with the loss of one's family would be traumatic for anyone to handle. Jack could empathize with that. However, what Jack could not understand was how a mature person like Robert could lose his sanity and resolve his grief by taking the lives of three hundred innocent passengers?

Was an agency behind this action? Was it another government? The Anti-Terrorism Department had refrained all ground communication with SL502 and had taken over all the conversations.

Robert had been declared a terrorist and a bigger hell awaited him with the landing of SL502, scheduled two hours later in New Guinea.

*****

Sarah got up from her seat and pulled out her laptop bag from the overhead bin. She needed to keep her mind occupied positively, constructively and purposefully. Sleep was hours away. So much had happened in so little time, from losing Mike to imagined infidelity, to the door of death and back. She had to do something that would deal with the turmoil in her mind and bring her some peace.

"You are going to work now?" Jim was all snuggled up and was planning on catching a nap for a couple of hours. His eyes were burning. He had not slept the entire night. The events of the last few hours had left him exhausted, both mentally and physically. He was hoping that Sarah would rest too. She needed to sleep. And, that way, he could be closer to her.

"I am going to write," Sarah smiled, "something that I should have done a long time ago. I guess when you turn away from your purpose, you fall prey to all the distractions of the world. Nothing makes sense anymore because you have gone astray from who you were meant to be. I am going to write the last chapter of my book." Sarah announced proudly for Muttu to hear too.

She switched on her laptop and braced herself to open up the folder she had titled 'Scribbles'. She had not given the book a name as yet, and 'Scribbles' fit the lack of depth that her editor said she had.

She created a new document with the title, 'In The End—There Is Love'. She thought for a few minutes and Jim stared at the blank computer screen, waiting for the words to emerge.

He was peaceful and happy. He had always wanted to go to New Guinea and this would be a good break with a beautiful girl.

I guess everything happens for a bigger reason than is apparent, he thought to himself. Everything happens for a reason. And with Sarah as his main reason, he would have a fantastic story to tell his friends, when they would ask 'How did you both meet?'

Sarah's book was about a love story gone wrong. Like most authors, the story drew a great deal from her own life. Two people in love had now turned to strangers, wanting out. They started off with love and as the chapters proceeded, the love receded. She had reached the end where the once love-struck couple would now separate. How could she add depth to the emotion of ending something that had once been so beautiful?

Sarah started to type.

Why don't relationships last? Relationships don't last, purposes do. As long as the people involved serve their purpose of being in a relationship, the relationship will continue to grow. When people's purposes drift apart, so does the relationship.

Jane blamed Martin for her misery. She never stopped to think that she was the cause of it. She wanted to end her relationship because she didn't feel loved, she didn't feel that she was important. She often complained that what started off as a beautiful dream had now turned into a nightmare.
Martin blamed Jane for his misery. He didn't feel loved and he didn't feel important. Jane had been such a darling in the beginning and now he had difficulty even reasoning with her.
There was equal blame on each side—equal and identical. What Jane said about Martin, he said about her in different words. Neither stopped to think that they had become exactly what they hated about the other. How could they see that? They were only blaming. Neither of them was listening. When one blamed, the other defended and countered the accusation. And so the story continued like a ping pong video game placed on auto, where no one wins but the players get tired and want out.

That something had gone terribly wrong, both Jane and Martin knew. But what had gone wrong and at what point, they could not figure. Problems were solved by pushing them under the carpet or by not addressing them.

It was the classic case of solving one problem by creating another. If water is leaking from the ceiling, instead of fixing that leakage, one puts a cloth to soak up the water that is seeping through. Does that solve the leakage? Not only does it not solve the leakage, it creates another problem—the wet cloth becomes a host for molds and dampness. To solve that, one brings in a humidifier. The humidifier handles the dampness, but the molds lead to cough and respiratory infection. To treat the cough, the person starts on antibiotics and syrups. The antibiotics lead to the onset of arthritis and gastrointestinal problems. To handle that, the person gets into physiotherapy, starts off on painkillers and then mood elevators to feel normal with all the drugs weighing him down. His irritableness, which is a by-product of medicines, does not serve him at work. His performance becomes poorer and he eventually loses his job. His relationship with his wife suffers as he carries his personal and professional burden at home. His wife files for divorce. Then one fine day, he sits down to think 'How did I land up here?' Even in a million years, he would not be able to locate the source of his troubles to that leakage in the ceiling. He finds himself professionally burdened, standing in court, leaving the woman who had been his pillar of support, because he didn't handle one leak in the ceiling.

Sometimes a problem extends so far from the source that one can no longer connect the dots and reach back to the root of the problem. When a problem shows up, it is definitely solvable, but when it is ignored long enough, its multiplication from different angles leaves no visible solution anymore.

A true solution is that which solves the problem. A solution, which keeps the problem intact but gives a temporary illusion of resolve, is not actually a solution—it might even aggravate the situation instead.

When something goes wrong, doesn't matter how big or small, it needs to be handled and solved. Leave it unattended and it will gain momentum and size, getting more severe with time.

Non-expression is a dangerous approach. Express both love and disappointment. When someone is expressing themselves to you, acknowledge it. Sometimes disappointment becomes a necessary outflow to protect love, which is temporarily shaken up. If you don't express yourself, how will the other person know, especially when you are hurt? Don't leave it for the other person to figure out. Express it. Shunning it or leaving it unresolved will break two hearts.

Happiness has a pattern; it has a particular wavelength, and a certain characteristic. Be a student of happiness—it will be the best learning of this lifetime. Recognize the patterns that make you happy. Understand the state of mind that attracts happiness. Know and acknowledge the actions that go into creating it. If you do that, then you will know how to be happy. Often people have forgotten that state of mind. How can they give love if they don't know how to be happy? Then they look for love in others to feel happy with themselves. That is a parasitic relationship most people define as love.

There is so much grief on the subject of importance. 'I don't feel important' is the common woe of the lover in distress. Lack of importance is a symptom of low self-esteem, not lack of love. One feels important when one is productive. One feels important when one's actions are in alignment with one's purpose. Love for the sake of importance is an idle man's indulgence. 'Since I am doing nothing, I need you to make me feel important.' Your presence in the relationship is evidence of your importance. For if you weren't, you wouldn't exist in that relationship.

Acceptance is the key to love. It comes from understanding that what I have is what I want. If I am ill, it's because I want to be ill, for being ill, in some manner, serves me. Whether it is the additional attention or the freedom from work or whatever reason one falls sick for. It is a condition of self-service. Allowing people to be is granting them the freedom to be in whatever state that they choose.

Don't use people's weaknesses against them. Ask what they would like you to do, for they are expecting something out of their condition, and then do it. When my five-year-old niece was ill, I asked her, 'Would you like to be better?' she answered 'No,' She was sick because she didn't want to go to school and making her better would make her really sick.

When a loved one is hurting, don't use your resolve, use theirs. What can I do for you? The answer to that will help their condition and help you serve them. When Jane was upset, Martin sent her flowers; what she needed was a long reassuring hug. And when the flowers didn't help uplift her, he was upset that he wasted his efforts. And that's how the love dissipates.

Love is expressed with allowance. You don't have to set someone free—that already is too late a thing to do. If you have to set someone free, it is because you had caged that person prior. And if that is what you did, then setting them free means they will never come back. Who would want to take the risk of imprisonment again?

When you first met, you were free, free to fall in love with anyone you so wished. You chose that one person. Later, when that person slowly clips your feathers to ground you, all you want to do is fly away. Not because he is grounding you, but because that is what you were meant to do—fly. Therefore, it is important to know in that first meeting if your destinations are the same. For if they aren't, then clipping your wings is the only way of keeping you together.

"That is so beautiful," Jim sniffed. "If I were born ten years earlier, I would ask you out. I would take you dancing. I would ask your hand in marriage to be my wife for all my lifetimes to come."

"You want more lifetimes?" Sarah smiled. She liked Jim. She was flattered by his comments and continual compliments. His attraction seemed innocent to her. He was unlike any teenager she had met. For him, she was unlike any woman he had met. She could understand his attraction and affinity. He was young, but he had a maturity that most grown-ups lacked. Sarah was growing fond of him. Jim would make the brother she never had. He would make a friend she had needed to have.

"With you in my life, I want lifetimes," Jim looked at Sarah. "You write so beautifully. If the end is so beautiful, then I only wonder how the whole book must be."

Sarah blushed with delight. She wanted to hug Jim and adopt him.

"You don't lack depth, how can someone with such insight lack depth? If these are your thoughts, then how couldn't you see through the lie your editor told you? I don't think he even read your book. Can't you see? What you have written is precious; it is loaded with wisdom and compassion. Change your editor. He doesn't seem to be a good man," Jim's protective instinct cropped up.

Sarah only stared at him, speechless.

"I'm sorry I interrupted you, please write," Jim nudged Sarah's shoulder with his head.

"It's the last chapter and I am trying to save love. It's difficult to restore love when it is clouded with layers and layers of misunderstanding. I don't mean misunderstanding between two people. It is about misunderstanding oneself." Sarah drifted into a deep thought again and Jim did what a person in love does, allowed her to be.

*****

Robert was pounding the armrest of his seat. What had he done? He had just confessed to murder. Why hadn't he thought about the radio recording? He had switched off the radio at some point in the conversation with Tom, but he wasn't sure when. Tom had made a comment about the Vitamin C in the coffee. Moreover, he had confessed to his wrongdoing. Was the radio switched on at that point? *Was it switched off?* He couldn't think clearly.

Robert stared at the blue sky ahead. The Widget was at his tail. He could feel the vibration. He had practically confessed his crime to the general of the Anti-Terrorism Department. They were not stupid. They would have pulled out the cockpit recordings even before they sent the Widget to find them. He was perplexed on how had they managed to find them in the first place? The ATS was far more technologically advanced than he had known.

As soon as the plane would land in New Guinea, the Anti-Terrorism Squad would surround the plane. Everyone would get out and then he would be arrested. He would be put in a special cell meant for terrorists. He would be questioned by means and methods that he had only heard about and seen in movies. That's why terrorists choose to die rather than be caught. His motive of suicide would not be accepted as the only motive. He would be tortured for information that he didn't have. Was he working for an agency? Was a terrorist group behind his actions? Was it another government? Since that was not the case he would be tortured, till he could not be tortured any more and then be sent for a trial where he would be judged without his involvement, and end up with a death sentence or life-imprisonment.

What had he done? How could he be so stupid? Why did he need to commit suicide in the plane, taking others down with him? He could have been home right now, on his bed, going peacefully without bothering anyone else. However, it was a dormant anger that found its expression in taking others down with him. It was that repressed anger which he had towards the air force for treating human life with indifference. The air force only lost a pilot while others lost a friend, a son, a brother, a husband, and a father.

It was his repressed anger towards the irresponsible action of the teenager who killed his family that didn't deserve to die. Why is alcohol available for misuse? What good did it serve? How can one expect responsibility from someone who has lost his senses to alcohol? Don't drink and drive. Is a drunken man capable of following instructions or keeping his word or even remembering the law? While the fellow got two years of detention in a juvenile home, Robert's family was banished from the world. Is the government then responsible for allowing the death of many who fall victim to the irresponsibility that it allows? Is the government then a party to the murder?

There was a rage in his heart that had been waiting to erupt. It had now erupted with full force. How can one forgive when the wrong continues to exist? How can one move on when the path ahead is made of thorns that continue to make one's wounds bleed?

Since there was no justice and life was unfair, he would avenge his family by putting an end to this insanity called life.

"SL502, maintain altitude at twenty-five thousand feet," Lieutenant General Sanders commanded.

"Do you copy?" the voice crackled on the radio.

Robert knew that the Widget could not sustain flight for long, above thirty thousand feet. Its maximum operation level was twenty-five thousand feet. So Sanders wanted him in his tow.

If he didn't comply now, Sanders would know that Robert's lie had been busted. And even if he knew, there was nothing he could do. Robert held the fate of the three hundred passengers aboard. Even if Sanders knew that Robert had deciphered his scheme, he could do nothing to stop Robert from taking the aircraft and its people down.

"You are not in command," Robert spoke on the radio, "I am."

The radio went silent as Robert could clearly imagine the face of Lieutenant General Sanders and the face of the Chief of the ATS on the ground with his words.

"Landing in New Guinea is no longer an option," Robert declared.

*****

"How do you prepare yourself to die? How does anyone prepare himself to die and to let go? A man lying on the operation table is fighting for his life even if he is nearing his end. He hasn't let go, that is why he is on the operation table. At what point does a person say, 'I quit', and give up?" Paul asked Muttu.

Paul's mind was at war. He had wanted to know when he would die so he could sort his life out with the countdown. He wanted to know how much time he had left so that he could start making decisions in alignment with his calling. Now that he had found out, he didn't have the time for all that he wanted to accomplish. How could he have taken his life for granted? How could he have taken his time for granted?

"I know I am going to die. I must confess I am not prepared for it," Muttu inhaled sharply. "I don't know what the necessary preparations are," he smiled. "We should have some sort of training to embrace death," he laughed. "Death is such a taboo subject that it upsets the person about to die as well as the people who watch him die. I have been preparing for this day since I was six and I must say that I am still not ready," Muttu let out a louder laugh.

"I must tell you, I really don't know what to do at this moment. What I do know is that I am not afraid to die. I am not sitting here in fear that my time has come. I know it will be up soon, but that does not frighten me. It does not disturb me.

"When I got on board the flight, I knew this was the end for everyone on board. However, for the first time, I wanted to be wrong. You know that feeling, when being wrong makes you right? When your baby girl is trying to arm-wrestle you, and you lose to her on purpose, so that she can win? You know that feeling?" he asked Paul. "So I asked Sarah for her date of birth. I wanted to be wrong, for her sake, for Jim's sake, for your sake, and for the sake of others I haven't yet connected with. But then, dying couldn't be wrong. So many people dying every day couldn't be wrong, right? If it were wrong, it wouldn't continue to happen. It couldn't be happening from the beginning of time. There must be something right about it. You see?" Muttu's question was rhetorical and profound. Paul's mind was alive and racing, keeping up with Muttu's wisdom.

"I am not the body. This body is not me. Do you follow?" Muttu asked Paul. Paul was American and here Muttu's spiritual upbringing could clash with Paul's western outlook when it came to that subject.

"I understand you totally," Paul confirmed. "I have followed many gurus in India and have attended many spiritual discourses too. Though I must say, none of them sounded as real to me as you do, at this moment. Maybe, at that time, I was not prepared to absorb and accept. Maybe the time is right now."

"The paradox is whether I am using the body or is the body using me? I chose to use my body. The body follows the physical laws of this universe. It will perish as it was designed to. It follows that law as religiously as does every other organism on the planet. I don't," Muttu said pausing. He didn't want to continue blabbering if his talk was not making sense to Paul.

"How do you know you are not your body? It is easier said than felt. Is it an innate wisdom or something that you have been taught?" Paul asked. He was not spiritually backward at all, he was spiritually ignited.

"I can see the future. My body cannot. The vision of my body is limited to three miles approximately on straight land. So who sees the future? My body? My body can't. *I* see it. I am not the body. In the physical world, the future does not exist. How can I see that which does not exist? That itself is my distinction," Muttu spoke softly so as not to distract a purposeful Sarah, who was busy on her laptop writing the last chapter of her book.

"What has always gnawed at me is that if I am a spiritual being, why don't I remember beyond the birth of this body?" Muttu confessed and Paul leaned in as Muttu's voice turned softer. "Why don't I remember who I really am if I am not this body? Where have I come from? Where have I been? Where am I going? And why am I here? That's what eats me up and that's the answer I have not been able to find."

Paul was getting goosebumps all over. Muttu had raised questions that had been haunting him for months. He had thought he would look at them when he had the time to indulge in spiritual matters. *This* was his time for indulgence.

"There are spirits who contact me," Muttu continued cautiously. He didn't want to scare Paul, but Paul was beyond being scared now. On another day, he would have taken the liberty of writing him off as crazy, but right now he wanted to know all that he could know.

"These are spirits who have messages for their loved ones. They watch over them, protect them," Muttu said.

"How do they contact you? How do you know it's a spirit contacting you?" Paul was curious.

"When I am sitting with a client, I sometimes start seeing them without any effort of my own. As though what I am seeing is shown to me. And when I relate it, that message is just what that client needed to hear," Muttu explained.

"What I am trying to say is that there are spirits who roam free without a body. I am curious about that. Imagine if I didn't have a body, I wouldn't have to bother to die," Muttu chuckled at that thought and Paul brightened up.

"So what are you going to do when your time comes?" Paul asked.

"I will leave. I will roam free. I certainly don't want to come back again to pick up another body. It's quite a hindrance if you ask me. I want to see the past, the present, the future, all at the same time. Heck, I don't want a past or a present or a future. I don't like this concept of time. I would like to indulge in eternity and move outward, into forever.

"I want to be and hold in me all there is. Like the sun that supports and sustains in it our whole solar system. What does it do? It is still. However, it holds in it a system full of action, you and me and this Airbus included," Muttu smiled and Paul laughed. Muttu made the business of dying an adventure.

"And this time around, I want to figure it all out. The answers are not found in serving the body again and again, one lifetime after another. I have a suspicion that the answers are found out of this material context. If I had to find them here, I would have found them. The key is not in the drawer; I have looked there several times. I am going to look for it outside now," Muttu said thoughtfully.

"How would others know? Wouldn't you have to come back to tell? Would you want to do that?" Paul queried.

"Do others really want to know? Why should I come back to tell? When they raise the question, they will seek out the answer. That is a journey every individual has to take for himself. *Death will set you free,* try telling that to the next passenger and he will send you to hell for that," Muttu giggled.

Paul was silent. He was no longer looking at Muttu. Muttu sighed and let the silence do what it does best, evoke reflection and introspection.

Minutes passed by and Muttu turned to Paul.

"Your son admires you a lot. He doesn't tell you that, but he tells others. He always wanted to be as good as you, but he felt he was not worthy of your attention. He held himself back for he felt that he would disappoint you, for you were the epitome of perfection for him. His life will change after you die. He will follow your footsteps and step up to the responsibility that you will leave behind. And he will do well. He will do you proud.

"Your ex-wife thinks of you every day. Not a day goes by that she does not think of how it would be if you both were still together. She could never be happy with other men because she always compared them to you. She never had the courage to come back to you because she could never forgive herself for what she did to you. Not for the things that you know she did, but for those you don't yet know.

"Your business will live, for your people are in alignment with your purpose. They will carry your legacy forward for they are proud of their contribution.

"Your best friend, Steve, will die two years from now. The cancer will make him suffer for many, many months. He will curse you for leaving so easily," Muttu smiled as Paul looked at him with tear-streaked eyes. For the first time in many years, he cried.

*****

"He went silent again? What's going on, Cathy? I don't understand." Glenda's fears crept back. Just when she had finished thanking the Lord, death raised its ugly head again.

"Why did you call the cockpit?" Cathy gritted her teeth with frustration.

"He called," Glenda defended herself. "He said we were landing in New Guinea. He said that Captain Tom tried to poison him and took the aircraft into the thundercloud and assaulted him. Captain Tom is dead," she repeated the story to Cathy.

The blood drained from Cathy's face. She knew something was wrong, but she had hoped that it was not to the extent of murder. It took her a few seconds to gather herself. How was Captain Joe involved in this? What had happened to him? Her gut churned, leading to a bout of dizziness. Knowing there is a murderer in the driving seat of your vehicle is terrifying. She had to remain calm. She had to stay in control.

Glenda stared at her in anticipation of an answer. Cathy was silent, but her mind was screaming at deafening decibels.

"What are we going to do?" Glenda was pacing the galley like a headless chicken. She missed Paul. His presence would have brought some reassurance in this situation. Glenda was fortunate that she was serving in first class. If she were in economy, she would have no time for tantrums and indulgence in frivolous matters, for the passengers would be demanding every second of her time. And Glenda being Glenda found no reason to offer help to her over-burdened colleagues in economy.

Cathy sat down. The story didn't make sense to her. Something was amiss. She didn't know what the truth was, but she knew this was certainly a lie. Tom did not seem like a man who was capable of murder. He looked more like a victim. When she saw him last, he looked like a man who was poisoned. Robert was the killer. But what could be his motive? Why would he kill his co-pilot? What was his intention?

Glenda raised her eyebrows at a silent Cathy. Cathy shook her head. She refrained from expressing what was in her mind; Glenda could not be trusted with anything.

She had to get Captain Joe out.

"Cover for me, I will be back," Cathy straightened herself up and began to walk out of the first class section.

"Where are you going?" Glenda asked in despair. First Paul and now Cathy. She did not want to be left alone.

"Do me a favour. Don't say anything to Captain Robert. Listen to him if he calls, but don't say anything," Cathy looked at Glenda and even though she nodded, she knew giving her instructions would be futile.

Cathy walked into the business class section and pulled flight attendant Brad aside. "The Captain is calling for you," she said, as the nosy flight attendants hovered around to see what had brought Cathy down from first class to business. She clearly wasn't there to help, for if that were her intention, she would have come down there long ago. Cathy was obviously not popular with her female co-workers.

Brad excused himself and followed Cathy. Cathy knew she could trust him.

"I want you to break open the door of the resting cabin. I know it's against policy and I am willing to take full responsibility. Captain Joe is inside, probably dead or ... murdered," Cathy didn't really have another explanation.

"What?!" Brad looked astonished. That explained everything. If Joe was dead, it meant that everyone's life was in danger.

Brad rushed to the first class section. The old man on seat 2F had been silent all this time. He seemed oblivious to the death that loomed in the air. He hadn't made any noise during the turbulence and had not even buzzed the air hostess once for an explanation. He had witnessed that the fate of everyone including himself was in danger. He could see that the air hostesses were worried. The flight was unstable and was hit by lightening. He knew that this could be his end. It would take a very evolved soul to be in a state of acceptance of death or in ignorance of its importance. Either way, he seemed at peace.

Brad tried to shove the door, but it didn't move. If he had to break it open it would create a loud noise and that would bring caution to whoever wanted Joe dead and trapped. He had to be discreet.

Brad got the cutlery from the service galley and began to dig at the latch first with a fork and then with a knife, alternating with thumps with his shoulder. It took less than three minutes for him to get the latch to turn.

"Stay clear," he placed his hand on Cathy. "Get on the other side of the galley and watch out for my response."

Cathy wanted to go into the cabin with him, but she could see Brad's logic. Glenda stood terrified midway. Cathy caught her arm and led her to the other side of the galley, pushing Glenda into Paul's seat.

Brad opened the door cautiously, prepared for an attack. He saw the feet of Captain Joe on the chair and took that as a clear sign and opened the door. He gulped at the sight of Captain Joe. The hair on Joe's head was raised. His eyes were open and dried out with the blood vessels that had burst inside. There was a yellow dried froth on his half-opened mouth. Brad walked in and placed his hand on Joe's neck checking for a pulse. There was none. He was dead.

Brad turned around and let out a yelp. "Jesus! Cathy!" He was startled by Cathy, who was standing right behind him. She kept staring at Joe. He was a wonderful man. Cathy had known him for five years. He had helped her out not only with adjusting her flight schedules but also helped her personally with hospital arrangements when her mother was critically ill. He was murdered. Tears ran out of Cathy's eyes. Brad embraced her and took her out of the cabin.

"Wait," Cathy said, wiping her tears. She walked into the cabin and picked up the empty coffee cup that lay on the tray beside him. She took the cup and marched up to Glenda.

"You served him the coffee, right?" she confronted Glenda.

"Yes," Glenda looked confused.

"Captain Joe was poisoned. He is dead. Captain Tom was poisoned. He is dead. The only thing common between them is the coffee. Where did you get this coffee? How did you make it?" Cathy panicked. Had Robert poisoned the whole coffee machine?

"Who all did you serve the coffee to from this machine?" Cathy shook Glenda.

"You, Mr. Glenn, me, Captain Tom, Captain Robert and Captain Joe," Glenda blurted nervously. She suddenly felt cramps in her stomach. Had she consumed the poison? And then it hit her! It was the coffee that she had taken from the cockpit and served Joe. Glenda's hands began to shake and the tremors spread through her entire body. If that coffee was poisoned, then she had killed Captain Joe.

Brad caught Glenda as she turned pale and leaned against the wall in the galley. Her hands were cold and beads of sweat shone on her forehead. Cathy looked at her alarmed. *Are we all going to die?* She shivered at the thought.

Brad struggled with Glenda and half carried and half dragged her to an empty seat. He began to rub her hands and her arms to get the blood flowing. Glenda covered her face with her hands and started to howl and sob hysterically. Her wails were loud and Cathy started to rub her shoulders to calm her down. Glenda was in shock.

"I killed Captain Joe," she whispered between her sobs, and Cathy and Brad froze.

"I gave the same coffee to him that you had got out from the cockpit. It was the same coffee. I poured more into the same cup," Glenda was crying, sobbing, sniffing and stuttering, and Cathy could barely make any sense out of what she was saying. Was she the killer?

"Listen to me, Glenda. Calm down. You need to tell me exactly what you did," Brad held her face with one hand and held her hands in the other, trying to take control.

It took a minute for Glenda to breathe normally.

"When Cathy asked me to get coffee for Captain Joe, I poured fresh coffee in the same cup that Cathy had brought from the cockpit. If Captain Tom was poisoned with that coffee, then I gave the same coffee to Captain Joe. I killed him," she told the truth and began to hyperventilate.

"Calm down," Brad tried to hold her tight.

"You need to get out there. Go to Business. I will stay here. Don't tell the others yet. We cannot have the panic spread," Brad said urgently to Cathy.

"We have a killer in charge of the plane. I cannot leave you here alone,"Cathy held onto Brad.

Brad put Cathy in charge of Glenda. He picked up the satellite phone and swiped his credit card. The signal and the connection, which had been off all this while was on now. Robert obviously hadn't planned this for he was leaving out finer details of the plot, which would lead to his doom—the satellite signal was on. He looked up the number on his phone and dialed Air Traffic Control. The phone rang.

"Pick up. Pick up," he muttered.

"Air Traffic Control," the lady at the board line chirped.

"Please put me to the Flight Control. This is Flight Attendant Brad calling from SL502," he hushed. "Hurry."

The lady at the switchboard looked at her nails, checking out her nail polish, and transferred the line to Flight Control.

"Flight Control Department. Henry speaking, how may I help you?" the voice finally came on after a few seconds of silence. "I'm Flight Attendant Brad aboard SL502. This is to report that Captain Joe has died of poisoning. Captain Tom is dead too. The killer we suspect is Captain Robert, in charge of the flight. The coffee was poisoned, which was consumed by both the captains," Brad explained.

"Listen Brad, the ATS has taken over. The situation is being handled delicately. We are bringing you down in New Guinea. Try to keep low and stay out of the captain's way. We will keep the line in check," Henry instructed and hung up.

"Who are you calling?" Cathy asked, as she walked up to Brad.

"Flight Control Department to report Captain Robert as the assassin. They have to be informed," Brad answered. Cathy's face went white with horror.

"The satellite phone is connected to the radio in the cockpit," she mumbled to Brad.

*****

"SL502, do you copy? Lower your altitude to twenty-five thousand feet," Lieutenant General Sanders did what the military are trained to do, repeat the command until executed, ignoring any signs of non-compliance.

Robert was long past rational thought. He was being set up. The ATS knew he had killed Tom and now with Brad's phone call, it seemed that the murder had been decoded. It was a simple case. Robert had been the stupid one thinking that he could get away with it.

"SL502, do you copy? Lower your altitude to twenty thousand feet," Lieutenant General Sanders repeated.

"Shit!" Sanders muttered as he got the message from ground control on the phone call from Brad. He knew that the satellite phone was connected to the cockpit. Robert knew that they knew he was the assassin.

"Shit!" he cursed again. "I had him! I had him!" he pounded his fist on his leg in frustration.

The Widget backed off, flying low at twenty-five thousand feet, keeping the Airbus in view. Although the aircraft was spanning the Pacific Ocean headed towards New Guinea, it had no intention of landing there.

*****

Sarah thought about Mike. Her relationship with him had already come to an end—for when there is no more trust, there is no relationship.

She continued to write.

How does one establish trust? Trust is merely an agreement of values and ethics the relationship will be run by. If I have agreed to a code of honour then, in breaking that I will break the trust. Often the honour is assumed. Marriage vows are exactly that. The priest reads out the code of honour and the couple is announced husband and wife when they agree to abide by it.

If the priest says 'Do you promise to stand by Jane in sickness and health,' and Martin says 'No, I won't be by her side in sickness,' the relationship ends there. When they agree to a code of conduct, they agree to honour that promise. Breaking that is a violation of the trust and should be taken seriously.

The start of a relationship should have a code of conduct. It should carry the values of both for each could have different values.

Do you agree to bring me flowers every Friday?

Do you agree to hug me when I am upset?

Do you agree to remain loyal to me?

Do you agree to listen when I am hurting no matter how unreasonable my plight may be?

Do you agree to forgive me if I don't behave myself sometimes?

Do you agree to love my dog?

Do you agree to give me space when I need it?

Do you agree to pursue asking me what's wrong even when I say I'm all right?

Either then the person says 'I do', or you negotiate. Once established, maintain the trust. It's easier to live in a relationship where the promise is established. People come from different experiences and different upbringings. What is okay with one may not be okay with another. Taking trust for granted is hanging your relationship on a fragile thread of misunderstanding.

To state clearly what one expects, entails a high understanding of one's own self. And when one understands oneself, it is very easy to understand the other.

Suspicion leads to wrongdoing. In suspecting the other, you are led to actions of blunder. Confronting is a better bet. Instead of burning in doubt, it is better to bring up the concern. Lying in wait for the person to mess up and catch him red-handed is worse than having a heart surgery. For when you win, you also die.

Sarah let out a long sigh. She shut her laptop to stop and think. Jim had fallen off to sleep. He was a playful teenager, eager to grow up. He spoke his mind and didn't hesitate to express. It was easy to like him, to become fond of him. Sarah smiled at his innocence.

Trust is where she was failing in her relationship with Mike. She couldn't trust him. Then why was she spending her time with him? What purpose did Mike serve in her life? She didn't have an answer. What purpose did she want him to serve in her life? She didn't have an answer.

She snapped open her laptop and typed again.

What is love? Attraction is not love. Attraction forms the basis of love. If you are attracted to the person, then there is a chance for love to grow. If there is no attraction, then there is also no love. For most people, love stops at attraction. And for most people, disaster follows after that.

If the attraction is purely physical, then love is a camouflage for lust. The attraction must be at all levels, emotional, mental, intellectual, spiritual AND physical. If I like how he looks, but I don't like how he thinks, then how long does one honestly expect the relationship to last? If I like how he thinks, but I don't like how he restricts himself emotionally, then how will love bloom? If I like his intellect but not his mentality, then what future awaits us both? Falling in love is like winning a jackpot—all the numbers should match. Even if there is just one number missing, you do not get the prize!

Sarah started to laugh. With Mike, many numbers had been missing. No wonder she was miserable. No wonder he was miserable.

She tapped the keyboard and then started punching again.

So how does one right the wrong? How does one correct a wrong choice once made? What does one do with a lottery ticket with the wrong numbers? How can one use it to win? One can't. One has to get a new ticket!

Sarah started to laugh out loud. It began as a soft chuckle and ended in full-blown laughter. Her love-life was such a shattered mess and she found it all so funny. The pain was gone; the heartbreak had found a release in her words.

Muttu looked at her and smiled. He didn't need to know what had amused her for her laughter didn't have the energy of a joke; it had the force of a truth realized.

*Looking at where one went wrong relieves the other person of the need to defend his stand. You invited him into your life; you gave him permission to mess you up. In other words, **you** chose him despite your better judgment, on poor intentions. Any way you look at it, you did it.*

Letting go is sometimes a better way, but doesn't have to be a cruel way. Let go, not because you hate the person or because it hurts. Let go because you want to create a better future.

Jane and Martin got together on the wrong numbers. After the attraction had died out, the other numbers came into view. Martin wanted to travel the world; Jane wanted to stay in her job. Jane wanted a big wedding; Martin wanted to marry in court. Martin was a party animal, Jane liked to stay at home. For Jane, Martin was her world, for Martin there was a world beyond Jane. As these numbers came to view, the truth emerged, that they had lost. Then each tried to unsuccessfully change the other, which only added to the misery. Try making a 3 into 8 and then go to the lottery office to claim the prize. That's cheating as they call it. So they begin to cheat, to make 8's out of the 3's with the people that they love.

Let go. Get another ticket.

Love isn't a lottery where you don't know what your fate is, where winning is not in your hands. Attraction at all levels is your key to hitting the jackpot. Compromise in the beginning and be ready for heartbreak later.

So how does one attract the right partner? How does one find him or her? By knowing what to look for. If you are clear about who you want, then recognizing the person becomes a lot easier. When you aren't clear about whom you want in your life, then your mood decides your selection.

While you are looking for your soulmate, keep yourself busy and keep yourself productive. It is always a good idea to estimate what kind of woman your dream man would want and prepare to live up to that standard. It's easy to expect the best and not consider what you have to offer in return. You want a hot guy? That's great. But also work at getting yourself in shape. For a hot guy such as your dream man is also looking for a hot woman. You want someone who is emotionally stable? Work on your own emotional make-up. He deserves the sanity as much as you expect it. You want someone who is spiritually evolved, find that in yourself first. And even if you don't find him soon, you will love yourself while you wait. It is when people stop loving themselves that they become desperate to find it in others. Desperation leads only to despair.

While you are looking for your soulmate, don't shun those who don't fit the bill. When you find someone intellectually stimulating, share that space with him. When you find an emotionally stable woman, include her in your list of good friends. When you bump into someone who is spiritually grounded, keep him as your philosopher and guide. When you meet a man who is physically attractive, be his friend, for not many women are. And when you find them all in one man— marry him, fast.

Sarah felt a surge of energy penetrate her heart, a healing energy. She had gotten on the flight with darkness in her soul and as the words poured out, they filled her with light. She was meant to take this flight, not because she wanted to find out the truth about Mike, but because she had to find the truth about herself.

She looked at Muttu, who was looking at her intently. "Thank you," she whispered and he beamed with pride.

THE RESOLVE

Robert's mind was a battlefield. He needed to think straight. He needed to evaluate his options. He was a dead man waiting to die.

Only two possibilities awaited him in the future. When a man has cut down the possibilities of his life to only two options, he is a dead man. For a man who is free, possibilities are unlimited. When someone says he has no options, he is dead in that context.

No matter which way Robert moved, he died. He had reached a 'checkmate'. Either the ATS would kill him slowly but surely or he would kill himself first. The only decision he had to make was, did three hundred people have to die with him?

Robert flung his seat belt open and got up from his seat. If he could just retrieve the capsule from the cavity, it would solve all his problems. But it was lodged so perfectly, as though the cavity were designed for it. The cavity was two inches deep, and there was no way he could reach it. It would have to be sucked out with a vacuum.

"Captain Robert, do you copy?" It was Lieutenant General Sanders again.

"I want to negotiate, do you copy?" the voice came in through the radio. Lieutenant General Sanders was happy that Robert had not cut off the radio this time. This meant there was scope for negotiation. The situation was akin to a man on the ledge, who is threatening to jump, but hasn't jumped as yet. There was still hope.

Frustrated, Robert got back to his seat. What negotiation could Sanders possibly offer him? It was all over. Any hope was only a façade to bring him down.

"Captain Robert, do you copy?" the command came in.

"What can you possibly offer me? I am a dead man, Sanders. Back off," Robert spoke into the radio.

"Get the plane onto the ground. I am willing to negotiate," Sanders came in.

"I get the plane on the ground and you will kill me, that's a guarantee," Robert spoke. In a very strange way, he was relieved to speak to someone. In speaking out, he didn't have to be a victim of the voices talking in his head.

"What do you want Robert? What do *you* want?" Sanders got straight to the point.

"I want to die. There is no other option," Robert said. It was true. There *was* no other option for him.

"Is that what you want, Robert? You want to die? Or is it that you want to die because there is no option? You don't have to die. Neither do the three hundred passengers aboard," Sanders tried to get to Robert. Colonel Jack was listening in from the ground, his fingers crossed. He had faith in Sanders. He had successfully negotiated and warded off many terrorist attacks. He was the best officer the air force had to offer.

Robert was confused. Did he hear correctly? Did Sanders just say that he didn't have to die?

"I don't understand. What do you mean by, I don't have to die?" Robert asked.

"I can get you immunity from the President. You land the plane and no one will touch you. You go underground, disappear, change your identity and never return to the United States. I can get you that immunity," Sanders negotiated.

Robert hadn't thought of that. Although he had no direct experience with terrorist negotiations, he knew that in times of extreme crisis where the lives of many were involved, the President had the authority to offer immunity if the terrorist in question agreed to surrender and cooperate. They were then declared dead to the public and banished from the country on a different identity.

A third possibility now opened up for Robert. He did not have to die. A little surge of hope flickered within him.

But what if Sanders was lying? What if he didn't get him the immunity promised and sent him to the torture cell instead? Did he want to take that chance?

"Negative, Sanders. I decline your offer," Robert spoke into the radio.

"The man is insane," Colonel Jack banged his fist on the table. He and his entire team were listening to the conversation from the ground. "The man is freaking insane!"

"I want to negotiate, Robert, for the lives of the three hundred passengers," Sanders changed his strategy. Jack took a deep breath and held it for Robert's response.

"Get the plane on the ground and I will personally shoot you. You will have your wish and the passengers don't have to die," Sanders voice crackled in through the radio.

Robert went silent. He thought about it. Would Sanders really do it? How could he know for sure? He knew that the stakes were high, and the negotiating officer will say everything you want to hear to get you to comply. There was no guarantee that those offers would be valid after the arrest.

"Negative, Sanders. I decline your offer," Robert stuck to his insanity.

There was silence. Both parties were thinking hard while a hopeful fleet of passengers waited in anticipation to get home, blissfully unaware of the crisis in the cockpit.

"What is your proposition, Robert?" Sanders' voice had mellowed down.

Robert was silent. That was the exact question he had been asking himself, ever since he got on the flight. What am I going to do? With every passing hour, he was getting deeper and deeper into trouble with that question. What could he possibly do?

"I am taking the plane down into the sea," Robert affirmed.

*****

"Will we make it?" Cathy asked Brad, who was seated with her in the galley. Glenda had fallen asleep on the seat in first class as her hysteria settled.

"We can only hope," Brad squeezed her hand.

"I wanted to quit flying last year. But I thought I would do one more year and then resign," Cathy said. "I wanted to play the guitar and form my own band and make music for a living. I needed another year to create a financial buffer before pursuing my dream," she paused. "When we land today, I will send in my resignation, and take a boat back home," she laughed and Brad joined in.

Talking to Brad was a relief and a big distraction from the fear that was constricting her heart. With two dead people in your space, it's hard to be normal. Cathy was trying hard.

"It's funny how it takes a crisis to shake us up to pay attention to what is really important." Brad picked up the conversation. "We take our life for granted and then we regret not doing that which we wanted to do most."

"Did you always want to fly?" Cathy asked him.

"I *always* wanted to fly. I feel I own the skies. Being up here gives me a high, literally and metaphorically," Brad smiled. He was happy that Cathy had trusted him, and he could be of help.

"Has this been your worst experience so far?" Cathy asked Brad. He had been flying longer than her. He had also worked in private jets, which are more susceptible to the dangers of flying than commercial airplanes.

"Well, what's the worst that can happen? Death? We all take that chance every day. Age is no longer a criterion for death. I wouldn't say this has been the worst experience, for I am an ardent fan of the silver lining. But yes, this has been the closest to death that I have ever been," Brad bent forward and then turned his face to look at Cathy.

"This has definitely been my worst experience ever. I thought I was going to die. I thought we were all going to die." Tears filled up Cathy's eyes.

"I'm glad that you lived to cry about it," Brad said, and Cathy broke out into a giggle before she could burst out into a sob.

"I'm glad you are here. It makes me feel safe. Thank you," Cathy breathed a sigh of relief.

*****

"Captain Robert, do you copy? I want to negotiate for the three hundred lives on board," Lieutenant General Sanders came on the radio again.

Robert remained silent. There was no negotiation. Why didn't Sanders understand that? There was no way out. His decision was made.

"For God's sake, Robert. You can die as you wish. However, all the three hundred don't need to die with you," Sanders came in again.

"Negative. I do not want to negotiate," Robert said, frustrated with the situation. He pushed the throttle forward a few inches, dipping the aircraft into a descent.

"Are we landing?" Cathy frowned. She looked at her watch. There was still an hour to go for New Guinea.

"SL502 losing altitude," Sanders shouted urgently to ground control.

"Do something, Sanders!!" Jack hollered, spilling his cup of coffee.

"You keep one passenger hostage in the cockpit. Land and sit in the cockpit. I will shoot you personally. You die. Everyone else lives," Sanders spoke with a sense of urgency.

Robert closed his eyes. His mind was racing. This plan could work. He could call Glenda in and hold her hostage. He would have her sit on Tom's seat so as to give a clean shot to Sanders. That could be the end.

But what if she struggled? She would see Tom's dead body and freak out. Why would she sit in the cockpit? He would have to assault her to keep her there. What if he buzzed for Glenda and she came in with a weapon—a knife or a fork or who knows, a blade, and attacked him first? They could then get instructions from the ground control and execute an emergency landing. He would then be thrown in the torture cell.

"Negative. I decline your offer," Robert had no way out. He wanted a way out, but he couldn't find one that would bring peace to his raging heart.

Robert looked at the fuel tank. He had another six hours to go, and after that, whether he wanted it or not, they were all going down. What was he waiting for? What does a dying man wait for?—Some extra time. He steadied the plane.

"Descent stopped," Sanders reported back to ground. Robert was one of the toughest cases he had ever encountered. How does one decipher the mind of a criminal? How does one influence the actions of a person who does not respond to reason?

Sanders remained silent. Something had occurred in Robert's mind for he had steadied the aircraft.

"Captain Robert, this is ATC, do you copy?" Jack took over, to Sanders' dismay.

"Captain Robert, this is Colonel Jack here from Air Traffic Control. Do you copy?" the voice came in over the radio.

Robert was taken by surprise. What did the ATC want when the Anti-Terrorism Department had taken over? What trick did they have up their sleeve now?

"What do you want?" Robert questioned.

"I have someone here who wants to speak to you," Jack spoke. Sanders cursed in the seat of his plane. He had told ATC to stay out of this, and now they were ruining his negotiation.

Robert was silent.

"Robert," a woman's voice came up on the radio. "This is Captain Fay."

The hair on Robert's body stood on end. Captain Fay was his dead wife's best friend.

*****

Mike was a nice guy. Sarah could see that. He was one of the most good-looking guys she had ever dated, and that had made her very insecure. Mike was popular with women and they managed to sway him even when he tried to remain loyal. The high that flirting brings, makes it a daily habit for some people. Individuals like Mike are highly sensual. That didn't make him a bad person; it made him different from what Sarah wanted in her man.

Mike was trying hard to change his ways. Not because he wanted to change, but because he didn't want to lose Sarah. Sarah was a nice girl, beautiful and very talented. She brought the much-needed stability to Mike's life. Unlike other women, he could see a future with her; he wanted to have a family with her. Her work made him proud. She was intelligent and she was sensible. But Mike just couldn't help himself when the attention from the opposite sex was constantly invading his space. Sometimes, he would refrain from indulgence; sometimes, he would pray that Sarah shouldn't find out. Sarah's work kept her travelling and that worked out just fine for Mike.

Mike and Sarah were struggling to save their relationship. They were poles apart in terms of attitude, each trying hard to be what the other wanted them to be and failing at that. They were good people, but they were not good together.

Sarah choked up. She opened her laptop, tried to overcome the hollow feeling that accompanies a sense of loss and began to type.

Instead of killing each other by changing them, and changing them, and changing them, and then making them feel guilty about who they are, it is better to let go. It is better to leave them to find their individual happiness than to suffocate them with your love.

Before you tear your heart apart, prepare yourself with the antidote. The best antidote to the fear of losing, the fear of being left alone and whatever fear it is that keeps us living small and loving smaller—is a compelling purpose. Define what makes you happy, explore your strengths, consider what you would love to do, and then construct a future with it. Purpose is a potent solution to all the ills of the mind and heart.

What did Sarah want to do with her life? She paused to think about it. What would she spend her life doing that would fill any gap that the loss of Mike would create? Sarah would write books. She would work on getting this one published. And if no one took it, she would write another one. She had something to share. When she wrote, it eased her heart, it brought her clarity, and it made her happy. If her writing did that for her, then maybe it would do the same for the reader. She would not allow others' judgment to define what she would do with her life. Her dreams were alive, and she was excited about her future.

What is the big deal about letting go? We fear it so much that we would rather suffer than face an alternate future. We fear that when the relationship ends, love will die, but love does not need to die. The context of a relationship can change, the love remaining constant. Love is the constant and does not necessarily need a relationship to hold it.

Even if people don't physically kill each other, time will kill them anyway, one sooner than the other. That it will all end is the truth about everything, about everyone. But must it end? My grandmother was in love with my grandfather, even after he died. She never married again. Many men vied for her, I heard, but she was in love with my grandfather. Need for physical intimacy is not love. Need for financial security is not love. Love transcends all needs. Love is what you feel beyond any physical evidence of its existence.

Instead of moving in with another man, my grandmother moved towards her purpose. She was a singer, a philanthropist and an exemplary mother. She indulged in her art and touched the lives of the listeners when she sang. She helped the unfortunate and the needy who blessed her abundantly. She brought up my mother and my uncles with pride and with grace. She was their hero. She spoilt us all with her love, and her humour. She never tired of telling us stories about her husband. She never let my mother feel his lack, for she never felt it herself. My grandfather's love surrounds us, as though he is still around, as though he is still with us.

In the end, if your love empowers those you claimed you loved, if your love brings hope and inspiration to their lives, if your love surrounds them long after you are gone, then you have truly loved.

Sarah began to breathe heavily. A relief engulfed her space. This was her closure. This was her letting go. She raised her arms and arched her back, stretching herself in the seat.

"Is it done?" Jim asked sleepily.

*****

"Robert," Fay's voice was stern.

"Damn it," Robert muttered. Captain Fay was his wife Karen's best friend. They were childhood friends and had always been together. They called themselves soul sisters. After his wife died, Fay had helped him get back on his feet. Robert wanted to stay away from her though; she reminded him of Karen. So Robert did all he could to avoid her. Recently, she was off duty from flying and was volunteering on the ground.

"Robert, I know you can hear me!" Fay said desperately.

"George is on your flight," she spoke in a voice choked with emotion.

Robert was shocked. Fay's husband was on his flight? Robert knew George. He was a brilliant lyricist and wrote some of the most popular jingles on TV. He was a creative genius. George was on his flight? He couldn't believe it.

"I am three months pregnant, Robert," Fay said into the radio.

Robert was silent. George was like family, and so was Fay. What had he done? What was he doing? What should he do now?

"Congratulations is what I would have expected," Fay scoffed.

"I don't know what has happened to you, Robert. I hear you want to kill everyone on board, my family included," she choked again.

Sanders was listening in. If this didn't work, nothing else would, he thought.

"I know you will kill everyone. What will I tell my child when he is born without his father? That he was murdered by my best friend's husband? That he was a victim of hate? What should I teach him—that between good and evil, evil wins? Is that what he should learn? That evil is more powerful, for good people lose?" Fay was on the verge of a breakdown.

"My baby is with me at this moment, hurting with pain. My unborn child is praying for the life of his father. Bring my husband home, Robert. Please!" Fay broke down into tears.

Robert remained silent.

"Say something, damn it!" she screamed into the radio.

Robert didn't know what to say. He had lost the courage to say even a single word to her.

"You are taking them all down aren't you, you bastard!" she yelled into the microphone.

"What you are doing is evil. Evil is never a choice, for to choose, one also needs to have a streak of goodness. When it comes down to an evil act, the goodness has long past gone. You are not just taking three hundred people down, you are taking their families down as well. Families that will have to live with what you did. The evil in your actions will remain with them. They will become it. Like you have. You are taking three hundred down, they might take three thousand down. A drunk driver killed three in your family; you are trying to get even with three hundred.

"Robert," Fay paused. "Don't do it," she broke down and sobbed.

"How can society value goodness when people like you make it a joke! If this is who you were destined to become, Robert, it's a good thing your family died and didn't live to see who you have become," Fay broke into tears and hit the microphone with her hand dropping it off the table.

"Leave me alone," she screamed at officers who came to hold her. She sat down in the chair as she and her unborn child wept for the husband and father they may never meet again.

*****

Muttu looked at his watch.

"One hour to go," he let out a long sigh.

"Are you nervous?" Paul asked.

From 'are you afraid' to 'are you nervous', the question marked a subtle spiritual progress.

"One hour to go," Muttu smiled. "I am glad that I am here, all locked up at thirty-five thousand feet. So I can do nothing at all," he let out a short laugh. "I like it. Doing nothing," and then he laughed again.

The satellite connections had been switched off so there was no option even to make that 'last call' to someone. When your time is up, often, there is no time left for wrap up. Paul, like Muttu, had nothing that he needed to do. They had done everything a long time ago, and that 'everything' had still made their life seem incomplete.

"How does one die? Is dying a doing or does it just happen?" Paul asked. He had gradually developed the certainty that Muttu knew all the answers. At least, he hoped that he did.

"Well, I don't really remember how I did it the last time around," Muttu laughed again, "but I can make an estimation on how it would be."

Paul smiled. Muttu's humour was catching on.

"According to my estimation," Muttu paused to look at Paul, "and I have given this a fair amount of thought," he nodded his head, "either your body dies, or your heart stops beating and you, as a soul, have no option but to leave. Or, you, as a soul, simply leave the body and allow it to die."

Paul frowned at his logic, "But that is exactly my question, *how does one leave?*"

"Well, we have an innate knowingness. No one taught a baby to suckle. No one taught a toddler to laugh. No one taught people how to have sex. No one taught you to be sad. When the time is right, when the circumstance presents itself, we know what to do," Muttu explained.

"What if I don't do it right?" Paul laughed at the absurdity of his question.

"Then you would be the only person whose complaint would be *'Darn, I didn't die correctly,'*" Muttu slapped Paul's shoulder, and they both laughed. It had all begun to sound amusingly ridiculous.

"You know, I am feeling a little light-headed," Muttu said beaming. "A mixture of euphoria, ecstasy and joy," he started to laugh, covering his mouth to keep it soft.

Paul was smiling but hadn't reached Muttu's state yet. He looked calm but pensive.

"So what about the tunnel of light and the angel or the God of Death waiting to take my soul?" Paul asked curiously. He wondered what Muttu's spiritual teaching said about that.

"If you ask me, I would avoid them," Muttu started to laugh again like one laughs in a state of light-headed drunkenness, "I want to be free really. I don't want to hang around the God of Birth and the God of Death. These are the two fellows who have gotten me into this trouble with the material world in the first place." He giggled again and this time Paul started to laugh as well.

"So we don't follow the light? Like they say you should in most of the religious scriptures?" Paul questioned.

"I don't know about you. I can't speak for you, but I am going to a place that makes me happy. Follow the light and go where? I don't know for sure where it leads. I landed up here again in a new body they call Muttu. I never felt free all my life. I want to *be*. I want to chill. I don't want to follow anyone or anything. This merry-go-round of birth and death has been going on for too long. I want to do my own thing now," Muttu said earnestly.

"Your own thing, like what?" Paul asked, intrigued. Muttu seemed to know what he was doing and Paul was going to tag along.

"Maybe explore another planet. Ours is becoming too polluted and corrupted. Or maybe hang around and help," Muttu stated in a matter-of-fact manner.

"Or maybe," Muttu came up with another idea, "just take a sabbatical from the material world and stay on as an observer."

"I like this idea better," Paul chipped in.

They fell into a comfortable silence. A small smile lingered on both their faces.

"What about salvation, Muttu? What about nirvana? I want freedom. I don't want to come back again and live at the mercy of destiny or a fate loaded with dualities. Will I be free after I die?" Paul was concerned.

"To be free, you have to move beyond the trap of Maya," Muttu explained.

"Maya? What is that all about?" Paul had heard about the Maya being attachment to materialism, but he wanted to hear Muttu's version.

"Maya is the deadliest weapon of the material universe. It is a Sanskrit word which translates into: "that which is not". It is an illusion that appears to be real. It is the illusion of mortality that makes matter real and the spirit obscure. Maya is why we are here in the body, wondering about a death that is not even real," Muttu looked intensely at Paul, gauging his level of comprehension. Paul was on the same page as Muttu.

"It is Maya that has trapped us here. Diminishing us as spiritual beings, making us unaware of who we really are, where we have been, what our purpose is, and what our abilities are. It reduces us to a life of servitude and struggle in the material world. Since that is totally against our innate nature, we suffer. Maya is the illusion of mortality.

"As long as you are blinded by that illusion, you are trapped. It's only when you can see beyond that lie, that façade, that trap, that you have a chance at freedom. Death is not freedom. Death is the beginning of a new game, back here on Earth, with a new body. You die as one body only to take on another. That's not freedom.

"You want salvation? You want nirvana? You want freedom? Just know who you are and be clear about who you are not! All your identities connected with the body are a lie. You are not a businessman. You are a power that is immortal and indestructible, a power force capable of assuming any beingness that you wish.

"You are not anything associated with matter. Your true place is a million light years away from this matter and this material world. Why would you need a body? How badly disillusioned you would have to be to believe you needed one to survive and to create! The trap set by Maya snaps shut when you, as a spiritual being, begin to believe that you are a body. When in the body, the illusion of Maya takes over, and you are trapped into the bonds and the laws of the material universe, which are contrary to your own innate nature and abilities. That is the final downward route for a spiritual being—to be consumed by Maya, by your agreement to be a body. For if you are matter, then it's easy to have you believe that you are mortal. When you believe you are mortal then you are afraid to die, you are afraid to lose. When fear creeps into the beingness of an immortal and indestructible soul, he is in full denial of his own self. That's Maya at work.

You are a formless, weightless nothingness, yet you are capable of enough power to create or destroy multiple universes at will.

"Awareness of your true self—therein lies your freedom. You have always been free. You have just forgotten who you are, by your obedience and adherence to Maya. The same Maya that embodies the lies that govern this material world," Muttu explained.

"You want freedom; remember who you are. Wake up. Wake up from this dream, this attachment to matter. You can see it in an instant if you wish or you can remain blinded for the rest of eternity. You chose not to see. You enrolled for the game. You made that choice at some point, for you couldn't be here without your consent to be here. You played willingly by giving up your identity. The choice has always been yours. You can choose to opt out and see reality. The Maya exists as long as you look outside and the material world is a big spread. The Maya is broken the minute you look within."

Paul heard him and had no questions anymore. He was looking for answers within; answers to questions that he had been reflecting upon for a long time. When he discussed his feeling of detachment from the material, his friends termed it as mid-life crisis. Paul was not becoming old; Paul was becoming himself, a spiritual being.

He sat back and closed his eyes. There were no prayers running in his mind. There were no thoughts. There was only a silence, which contained in it all there is ... said, unsaid, seen, unseen, felt, unfelt, known, unknown. There was no need for anything. It was a state of bliss. A state of nothingness, which nonetheless held in it, a sense of spiritual fulfilment. Paul was consumed by this state he had so yearned for. He knew this was exactly what he was looking for; it was exactly what had been missing all his life.

Time was ticking by. The clock was ticking backward on Muttu's wrist. It marked the countdown to the end, or to a brand new beginning. If they didn't understand and didn't enlighten to their own realities, to their own truth, they may serve another few decades in another lifetime, figuring out. It was now, or some other moment in eternity.

Whether Muttu knew what he knew in theory or whether he was enlightened enough to know from a state of spiritual beingness, only the end would tell. Whether Muttu had truly seen past the illusion or whether he was only preaching a well-rehearsed philosophy, the end was sure to reveal the verdict of a future entrapment or eternal freedom.

"Hey, Muttu," Paul said, turning to him after a few moments of silence. "The Captain is going to kill himself."

"How do you know that?" Muttu asked.

"I can see him. I can read his thoughts. He is very disturbed. He will kill himself," Paul said, "I can see the future."

Muttu nodded in acknowledgement. He knew exactly what Paul was talking about. Perception is not limited to the senses of our body. There is more to it. At the spiritual level, one would describe it as pervasion. Where you pervade space and you can know. You can pervade time and you can know the past, the present and the future. Muttu knew that this wasn't a special ability of a few; it was an ability common to all. That everyone had forgotten it was a different story. That everyone had the potential to reclaim their innate power was a story he believed.

"How did you do that?" Muttu wanted to be a part of Paul's evolution. He knew, but it's always a joy to know again, as it validates what you already know.

"I can see, not with my body, but, I can see with a perception which I always sensed I had, but never connected with. I feel overwhelmed, like you feel when you have lost everything, and in that losing, you free yourself. For that losing takes with it all the stress and all the angst and all the insecurity that came along with the urge to keep it, to possess and protect it.

"I had given everything away. The last thing left to surrender was the body. The minute I do that, I will be free. I am suddenly on a different level. I am still alive, but I feel no attachment to this body. You can take it, you can destroy it, you can do what you like with it, and that has no implication on who I am and how I feel about myself.

"How did I do it? I don't know. I just did. As though I just woke up. As though the truth just hit me. As though the lie just dissipated, leaving me with me," Paul narrowed his brows, searching in Muttu's eyes to see if he understood.

"You made it," Muttu whispered. He knew what Paul was talking about. Paul had summed up exactly what Muttu had been feeling for quite some time now.

Paul had seen that the captain would die and that had not changed his state in the present. According to Muttu, that was a spiritual state only a very few acquire.

"I can see the future, Muttu," Paul said, with certainty in the vision that he had just experienced.

"I can see the past, not as what I have experienced, for those are just memories. I can see the past, the past that encompasses the lives and journeys of everyone. I can see the present as a state that is created by everyone. And I can understand everyone.

"Even though I can see that the near future holds an incident of devastation for many, I have no need or urge to alter it. Wanting to change things is enrolling in the game again. To be unchanged in the face of any reality, good or bad, is a state I have now acquired.

"I can see the Maya, the illusion. It creates the illusion of mortality and reels you in. It creates riddles so you can play the game of solving them. It creates destruction and devastation, capturing your attention on setting it right. In that engagement, you get consumed with a negative force, fighting it till you can fight no more. The Maya wins when you lose. The Maya wins when you become it, like Robert has. He is a glorified victim. His actions are going to trigger others to be further entrapped in getting even.

"I can see, Muttu. I can see the lie. I can see the misery that the lies bring with it. I can see the trap. We are all trapped.

"I never saw it like this before. I knew I was suffering. I knew that life didn't make sense. I knew that the more I achieved, the less connected I felt with myself. I knew that I was not who I thought I was. I knew there was more to me. But I had already reached the pinnacle of my success. What more was there to be? That's where I was stuck. That's the answer I was after. I can see now. It's so clear. I am more than the material world ever allowed me to be. I am more than I was being. I am much more, Muttu."

Muttu smiled broadly. Paul was tuned in. Paul knew. Paul could see the Maya, he could decipher the illusion; he could see the truth about himself and about his eternity.

Muttu and Paul, they had become fellow travellers on the flight, in life and beyond.

*****

Robert dug his face into his hands and his eyes were swollen from crying. Years of holding back his emotions had erupted like an angry volcano. This is not who he was. This is not what he had wanted to become. If his wife and his daughters were here, they would be ashamed of what he had done. Then again, if his wife and his daughters were here, he wouldn't be doing this.

Robert got off his seat. He had to get the capsule somehow, anyhow. He looked at the cavity. It was impossible. Suddenly an idea hit him. He slapped his hand on his chest and unhooked his badge. He took the pin and bent it. He stuck the pin into the capsule, turned it inside, and then very slowly began to lift it out of the cavity.

In a few gentle tugs, the capsule came loose and hung on the pilot's badge like a fish caught on a hook.

He took the capsule in his palm and held it tight. This was his solution. He got back to his seat. He had to do this right.

The peddler had told him that if he consumed the contents sublingually, by putting the powder under his tongue, the poison would act much faster. With water it would kill him within a couple of hours or less; sublingually it would kill him in thirty minutes.

Robert began to think. This time he needed to plan correctly. He looked at his watch; if he wanted to land in New Guinea, he should begin his descent now. He had thirty minutes to land in New Guinea.

He began to lay out a plan in his head. He had thirty minutes. He would get the plane ready for descent. He would put the aircraft on autopilot. Twenty minutes into landing, he would consume the poison. He would land the plane and stop it on the runway. It would take the Anti-Terrorism Squad five minutes to get the plane open, that was twenty-five minutes. It would take them at least five minutes to evacuate the aircraft. That was thirty minutes. They would break open the cockpit and arrest him. By the time they would take him off to wherever he needed to be taken, he would be dead. If the poison took longer to kill him, they would try to give him antidotes to counter the poison. That's why he had obtained a combination of two poisons. It would take them one full day to figure the antidote after running the autopsy on the two dead bodies. Even if the poison took two hours to kill him, by the time the paramedics worked on him, he would be dead. The peddler had promised it didn't have an antidote but then peddlers aren't the most trustworthy people on the planet. Tom was dead, so he had evidence of the peddler's claims. What's more, Tom had only consumed half the contents.

This plan would work. Robert was satisfied. He straightened up in his seat, put his headphones on. He placed the capsule in his pocket and switched on the controls. He pushed the button to auto-pilot and studied the radar intensely. He turned the knob to adjust the altitude and speed to landing. Fay was wrong. He could still turn around. He could save the three hundred people so he could face Karen when he met her.

Robert flipped on the radio. "ATC do you copy?" he buzzed. "Prepare the airbase at New Guinea for landing, I am bringing the Airbus home."

A cheer broke out at the ATC. Colonel Jack remained unaffected by the news. He had seen too many erratic outbursts from Robert to believe what he was saying this time. It was Captain Fay who walked to the microphone and said, "Thank you, Robert."

Lieutenant General Sanders had gone silent. He had been counting on Fay's talk to have an impact on Robert, and it had worked. He was still tailing the aircraft lest it break connection again.

"Ladies and gentlemen, this is your captain speaking. Due to unavoidable circumstances, there has been a change in our route. We have begun our descent to New Guinea. We will land in approximately twenty-five minutes. The weather at New Guinea is pleasant. The temperature is about sixty-five degrees. We will be changing the aircraft and the ground staff will help you with your journey forward," he paused with the announcement. "Flight Attendants, prepare the aircraft for landing," he concluded.

A big round of cheer and applause rang through the aircraft. A few holy songs had sprung up among passengers, and many participated by clapping in rhythm as they thanked the Lord.

*****

Sarah packed her laptop away while the flight attendants started giving landing instructions. Jim had straightened up and was looking forward to spending a few hours in New Guinea with Sarah. He would look after her and ensure her safety.

"That was a close call," Sarah looked happy. "You know we could all have died today? Did you see the force of the lightning that went through the aircraft? It could have killed an elephant," she shook her head.

"Can I share a secret with you?" Jim looked at Sarah. "If I had to choose how I go, I would want to die in an air crash."

Sarah looked at him startled. Here was a seventeen-year-old boy telling her that he had thought about his death.

"What?!" she asked, alarmed.

"Yeah, I mean I don't want to die in a hospital where you are the only one dying and everyone is looking down at you with pity. Imagine how horrible you would feel knowing that all these people would live and you would be no more. At least when dying in a plane crash, I would have company. So no one would feel bad because everyone would die together," Jim chuckled. Sarah just continued to stare at him and then shook her head and patted his arm. She was amused with his views on life.

The point that Sarah was trying to make was that they could

have died. This close brush with death made her grievances with Mike irrelevant. She had a new life, a new perspective. She would watch out for Mike and continue to be his friend and continue to love him. There was no need for the love to end with the relationship.

"I am going to send my book out to publishers," Sarah affirmed.

"You have to send me a copy when it is published," Jim shared her excitement.

"Why? Won't you be around to share the joy?" She scowled. "Does it all end with this flight?" she complained playfully.

"I will be around. You can count on that!" Jim assured her. The intensity in his eyes gave more meaning to his words than Sarah wanted or understood.

*****

The plane was cruising low over the ocean. Ships and boats were becoming clearly visible now. The weather was inviting indulgence. It was a perfect day for surfing or a nap on the beach.

Robert looked at his watch. He had five minutes before he would take his poison. He would land the plane and then it would all be over for him. Life was not an option. Captain Tom, lying dead next to him, was a constant reminder that the countdown on his own life had started, even if he had wanted out.

He had messed up. The panic and fear that the three hundred passengers had felt during the five hours of the flight, he had felt that panic, that misery and that fear collectively for many months now. He sighed with relief that it was finally going to be over. He actually felt peaceful in an irrational way.

Robert stared ahead without blinking, lost in nothingness. Good memories from his life began to whirl through his mind. He had had a good life while it had lasted. He had been capable of love, he had been capable of kindness, and he had been capable of honour. This past one year had been a bad dream, and he badly needed to wake up.

The island was visible now. What time was it? Ten minutes had gone by. He was five minutes away from landing.

Robert began to panic. He took the capsule out of his pocket. This was it.

He slowly opened the capsule tapping the wall of the capsule so that its contents wouldn't spill out. He could not afford to mess up this time. He looked at the island ahead. It was about fifteen miles away.

He opened his mouth and tapped the contents under his tongue. The powder had a smoky taste. The powder triggered a flow of saliva as he felt the grains melt under his tongue. He looked at his watch. He had thirty minutes to live.

He waited for a minute. Nothing happened. Was it working? Nothing was happening? Robert looked at Tom. How long before the poison kicked in?

*****

On the airbase at New Guinea, the Anti-Terrorism Squad was ready. The Widget had already taken two rounds and would land in after the Airbus. The entire airport was empty. The runway was cordoned off. All roads leading towards the airport were blocked.

There were eleven military jeeps waiting just short of the runway with armed soldiers while others were in position around the entire airbase. Ten ambulances were queued up in line.

The US Air Force had made every possible preparation that could be made to ensure that three hundred people came out of the airplane alive.

*****

"We are landing," Paul knew the sound of the wheels opening up. He looked out of the window. The waters were clear.

"Yes," Muttu smiled.

Paul looked at his watch. At the same time, Muttu's watch beeped.

"It's time," Muttu smiled as he turned his wrist to show the numbers 00:00 to Paul.

"Then why aren't we dead?" Paul was confused.

"My watch is five minutes fast," Muttu smiled nervously.

*****

Robert kept moving his hands and toes to feel any onset of paralysis. There was no sign of numbness or any discomfort. The poison had melted in his mouth and had been fully absorbed. Why wasn't it working?
The plane was flying at fifteen hundred feet above the sea. The red lights of the ambulances at the airport were flashing into view.

"Oh God! Oh God!" Robert broke into a panic. Just then, as an answer to his prayers, a sharp dagger-like sensation sliced through his brain. Robert opened his mouth to scream, but the pain had stunned and paralyzed him. His hands were firmly clutching the throttle. He just needed to push it four inches down to bring the plane to land. He just needed five more minutes of control, and he would make it to the ground. His vision began to blur. Multiple islands began to dance in the distance. The control panel in front of him began to turn a shade of grey and then black. A severe cramp crunched his stomach twisting the muscles in his gut. Robert withered in pain. He felt his spine split into a thousand bony splinters. With one last gush of breath, his lungs squeezed the air out of his body.

Robert gasped. He tried hard to fight the pain and the blackout, to keep his focus on the land. He had to get the plane down.

Robert's reflexes were out of his control. His body thrashed to the left with a jerk and then lunged to the right. It was as though someone was jolting him from left to right. Robert's head began to dangle, and his vision turned upside down. His mind was alert, but his body seemed out of his control. Death had come to take possession of the body and was squeezing the life out.

A sharp pain pierced through Robert's eyes. He opened his mouth to scream, but his lungs had already collapsed. He first felt his body thrust backward and then with a big heave it fell forward, his head hitting the throttle pushing it all the way up.

"Nooooo!" Robert screamed a voiceless scream as the nose of the plane dipped forty-five degrees towards the sea.

*****

The sharp dive jolted all the passengers off their seats, with the seat belts holding their suspended bodies to the seats.

Sarah opened her mouth to scream, but the sound drowned half way into her windpipe. The sudden dip drove her, as it did so many others, into shock. Jim's hand grasped her shoulder.

"We are going to die! We are going to die!" Sarah broke out into a hysterical stutter.

Jim was holding on to the headrest of the front seat with one hand and was clutching Sarah with the other.

"I know," he murmured. "And I am going with you."

Paul's phone fell out of his pocket as his body was thrown forward with the tilt. With both his arms braced on the seat in front, his head was turned towards the window. All he could see was the ocean, speeding towards him.

"This is it!" he whispered. "This is it!" he shouted for Muttu to hear above the cries, sobs, and wails that were echoing through the aircraft.

Muttu's eyes were closed. His body was suspended comfortably by his seat belt. His lips were quivering with a chant.

Paul wanted to hold him. Paul wanted to talk to him. But Muttu was on his way, into an alternate future.

At the moment where one can see that the end is near, there is total helplessness. Screaming, shouting and protesting are all but futile actions then. There were tears. Not tears of pain, but those loaded with the fear of losing, with the fear of dying. A futile effort was exerted in averting the loss of the body and confronting death of the material body. The gods were being called upon for one last divine intervention. Prayers were offered to preserve the matter, to keep the curtain of illusion, the Maya tightly shut from the truth. But the gods were only doing what they do best—allowing the eternal spirits one more shot at the truth, one more chance to their own awakening, by letting them be.

With the sharp dip, the whole body of the aircraft flung upward from the tail moving in an arch perpendicular to the ground. The passengers were thrown forward, and suddenly a deafening silence prevailed. The plane then heaved back a few degrees and headed straight for the ocean, towards a seven-second fall into the Pacific Ocean.

The airbase at New Guinea watched speechless and stunned. The ATC general lost his voice as he held the microphone in his hand to make contact with the captain, but no words emerged from his mouth.

Time stands still at an extreme emotional moment such as this. Just like death suspends the body into nothingness forever, the emotion of ecstasy does the same thing. These were the last, and the longest seven seconds, in the lives of the passengers aboard the Flight SL502.

When the end is near, when the time is up—the spirit knows. No matter what one says, when you are facing the end of this road called life—*you know*. What do you do then? Does death need preparation? If you don't know how to die, does that mean you won't? SL502 carried three hundred people who knew. They knew how to live and they knew how to die, for they had done it several times over already. SL502 carried three hundred old souls back to where they belonged—their freedom.

$$*****$$

As the plane tipped further, the pressure built up in Muttu's head as the adrenaline spiked, in a last and hopeless attempt to protect the body from going into shock. Jim's hand was tightly on Sarah's whose body was shaking like a fish out of water, and in the next second, it went limp. Paul was alert to every moment, every minute motion, every heartbeat, every breath.

The next second marked a war between the body and the soul, the soul wanting to break free from the trauma that awaited the body a few seconds later, and the body holding on to the soul in hope of survival.

Jim could feel a convulsion emanating from Sarah. She would leave soon. He wanted to be there for when she did and then follow through.

The third second left the body in shock, as the soul tugged off its last alliance with the body, pulling itself out. When the soul rejects the body, it goes into shock, which leads it to its final death. When the body rejects the soul, it leaves the soul in a state of shock, with its attention hung upon the loss of the body and the world around it.

Eyes open, heart stopped, nervous system shut down, Muttu's body collapsed like jelly following the jerks and movement of the aircraft. Sarah was next to go slump like a plug had been pulled off a robot, collapsing it midway. Jim fell forward limp, his arm locked onto Sarah's dead body. Paul was the last to leave. A pang in his heart caused the arteries to explode.

The fourth second led to a rise, a detachment where the body fell down and the spirit rose up, free.

The fifth, sixth and seventh seconds were the longest, in a space where time is of no relevance, where stillness is a way of existence, where attention spreads out encompassing an understanding, an all-knowing pervasion.

One by one, the horror-struck bodies began to collapse, as though following the trail of the ones who had left. Each one wrapped up their material connection and set the spirit free, as if by instinct, on an innate knowing that the time for the body was up, and the time for the spirit to move on had started.

The nose hit the ocean first making a dent in the water where it collided. The water broke at the impact sending panic waves to the island. The aircraft tilted on its side. The left wing tore away from the aircraft on impact, releasing a gush of fuel into the ocean. The plane bobbed for a split second and then fell sideward on the water, one wing suspended in the air.

There was one body that was alive against its will, that was witness to death in its goriest glory—Captain Robert. His eyes and mouth were open. His spirit was too shocked, holding on for some divine moment of grace to save the aircraft.

The glass of the cockpit shattered with a crash, as the ocean entered, lashing with rage at Robert, to consume the madness that had prevailed in the cockpit for the last five hours.

SL502 floated for a few seconds, allowing people on ground to capture images that would haunt millions, for every flight that they would take, for the longest time. As soon as the tail hit the water, the aircraft began its speedy descent to the bottom of the ocean. In a few seconds, all that was visible was the wing that looked like the fin of a very sinister giant shark, and then it was gone.

Flight SL502 had crashed two miles away from the landing strip at New Guinea.

....

IN THE END – LET THERE BE LOVE

....

Skyline Airbus Flight SL502 sank like a rock to the bottom of the ocean. Three helicopters circled the air like hungry birds disappointed at the escape of their prey. The Widget flew to and fro at deafening pace in denial of its defeat.

A team of divers was released from the choppers to follow after the sinking Airbus. Their arrival within minutes came as a surprise to the spectators. The fire department, the air force and the navy seals are prepared for disaster 24X7. They had been standing by for this contingency hoping that the plane would land safely and they would not be needed.

The sinking created a strong whirling undercurrent towards the ocean bed, sucking the divers in the direction of the aircraft.

The Airbus hit the bottom of the ocean. A mud-cloud rose from the ocean bed, engulfing the aircraft and blocking it from the view of the divers. With the nose dug firmly into the earth, a few hundred metres below sea level, the aircraft creaked and groaned and finally gave into the pressure of the water and the centrifugal force. It split open from the center, breaking into two.

For miles, all eyes were fixed on the ocean as they stood witness to one of the deadliest mishaps of the decade. The crash of SL502 was a public spectacle.

*****

The silence lasted a few seconds and then the atmosphere

charged up with a dense spiritual presence.

"What the hell happened?"

"I'm dead!"

"We are all dead."

"Am I dead?"

"Am I going to hell?"

"Can anyone see the light?"

"Where's the bloody captain?"

The three hundred passengers aboard Flight SL502 were witness to the worst ever air crash in the history of aviation, where all three hundred bodies had died, and all three hundred souls had survived.

*****

"What's happening here?"

Confusion and chaos filled the air. There were three hundred souls that had been yanked out of their bodies. For a few passing moments, a feeling of loss, bewilderment and grief hung thick amongst them. The attention of most of these beings was stuck on the loss of their body. The atmosphere was weighed down with heavy emotion. There seemed to be a collective awareness of a failed purpose. All the intentions were connected with the body. With the body gone, the purpose was gone too.
Some beings went darting after their dead bodies, fixated in

a state of helplessness, unable to get back to their physical state, mourning its loss. Others went raging in all directions, something they had done in their daily lives when things didn't go as planned. Most of them just stayed there, suspended in time, still confused about what had just happened. They had not come to terms with the loss of their body or accepted their spiritual state without one.

"So …. are we all dead now?" someone raised the innocent question.

"Hey, I didn't have plans to die. I had an important meeting I had to reach!" a naïve soul complained.

"I was going to get married next week."

"I was scheduled for a knee replacement."

"I was going for my daughter's first theatrical performance."

"I had just bought a new house."

"It's not fair. All our plans thwarted. Our lives lost to the actions of one crazy man!"

"Where is the bloody captain? I will hunt him down and kill him!"

"But he's already dead!"

"Then I will spend eternity beating the hell out of him."

"Why waste your eternity in revenge!"

"He needs to learn a lesson."

"In teaching him that lesson, what would you have learnt?"

There were spurts of anger and stillness. The space was loaded with emotional charge.

The three hundred souls had gotten together on the flight for a reason— freedom, but not all of them were ready for it, yet. They each had yet another chance to recognize the futility of the material existence which they had left behind. However, not all were prepared to see that. Here they had another chance, in the guise of death, to be free, not just from the body but also from the bonds of materialism. These bonds kept them entangled in the lies of mortality, but not many were even looking for that chance to break free.

The huddle above the crash site began to thin away. Some beings went away searching in rage for the captain. Others dove towards their material lives, hovering over what used to be their home, their possessions, and their life. Yet some others found themselves purpose-bound to find their way back into the cycle of a new birth. They lined up to get new bodies, not because they wanted to be spiritually enslaved again but because operating with a body had become a habit, like a second nature. The material connection brought a security of familiarity. It was a game that they had played for so long that being players and being played upon was all they knew.

Amongst all of this spiritual confusion, there were a few evolved souls, special beings who had found each other on Row 26. These like-minded curious souls stayed on.

*****

It was a cloudless blue sky. There was a clear passage from the earth to the other worlds for anyone who wished to take that route to freedom. But there had been no takers, yet.

A rumble and a roar cracked around the ocean. It was Muttu.

His prediction had come true. He had seen the future and he had embraced it gracefully.

"Is that you, Muttu?"

"Well, that's what they called me in the physical world, but yes, it's me, Paul." A rumble was felt again as the two beings emanated electric energy, witnessing a transition from the material to the spiritual.

"It's gone. It's all gone. The body. The work that I had done. The empire that I had built. The family, the friends, the familiarity, it's all gone. And boy, do I feel relieved!" Paul expressed.

"Wow, I feel weightless, formless and yet so aware," Muttu exclaimed elatedly.

"Is this who I really am? I had to lose everything to discover who I really am. And here I am. I can see without eyes, I can hear without ears, I can speak without a mouth and my awareness transcends all boundaries. I am free," Paul rejoiced.

"What now? Where do I head? What do I do?" Paul went deep into reflection.

"That's what I have been trying to decipher all my life. None of the answers come close to what I feel at this moment. A relief beyond description," Muttu communicated back.

"Can you feel a strong wave of affinity close by?" Paul sensed a growing sense of love pervading their space.

"It's them," Muttu could feel the presence of Sarah and Jim.

"I found you!" Jim exclaimed with joy. With the barrier of the body and its rules gone, Jim could now see Sarah as the spiritual being that he had loved for all eternity. The affinity and the attraction that he had felt for her, ever since he saw her, had not been directed at her body. It was an inexplicable connection that had drawn him to her. The same connection, which had urged him to take this flight, to be with her in these last moments, which would lead to their union once again.

"I have been looking for you for so long. I have been looking for you in every person that I met. Trying to search for this connection, this bond that I share with you. I am so happy that I have finally found you," Jim's love was expanding, engulfing everyone who came close to his space.

"Why can't I remember?" Sarah was overwhelmed with the affinity that she felt emanating from Jim. He was much younger than her when in the body and that restricted and defined her feelings and her relationship with him. With the body gone, the ageless and timeless souls were united in the one feeling that is innate to them, love, and the one relationship that defines all spiritual relationships, co-creation.

A stillness allowed them much-needed space to recognize themselves for who they really were—something these beings had missed doing during their lifetime.

Jim allowed Sarah her space. As a spiritual being, he knew that he loved her and that was enough. Sarah had forgotten and that had no bearing on what Jim felt. Love is not defined by reciprocation. It is a feeling that emanates from who you are and touches those who come into your space.

*****

"The Captain is an assassin! That rat bastard! He poisoned me first and then the negligent air hostess poisoned Joe. The captain's insanity killed me mercilessly," Tom's wrath filled the space, disrupting the peace and the love these four evolved souls were experiencing.

"I followed the aircraft. I just wanted to ensure that it would land safely so others didn't have to be victim to his madness like Joe and me. But that maniac brought everyone down."

"How could you make sure the plane would land? You were already dead," Muttu tried to direct Tom's attention from grief and anger to his spiritual state.

"Don't you get it? The body needs force to create action whereas the spirit only needs intention. How are you communicating at the moment? You have no body, no voice, and I have no ears. Then how are we communicating? By intention. That's how I was trying to ensure the plane would land," Tom explained angrily. He was so consumed by rage that even though he was spiritually ignited, he could not see it.

"Is that how powerful you are? Even without your body, you can influence and control a plane?" Muttu tried to help him realize his fallacy. Holding onto negativity was a trademark of the material world and would pull one back towards it.

Tom was still hung up on the injustice that was done to him. He was totally missing the point, the truth about who he really was. He was fuming mad that he had been killed and he just couldn't see that that attempt was a spiritual impossibility.

A spiritual fury was brewing right above the site where its material connection, the physical bodies, were turning to mud. Many of the beings were engaged in a quest for vengeance. They were engaged in the same game that had trapped them in the material world to start with, 'you took my thing and now I will get even with you.'

"Hey!" Muttu brought Tom's attention to the present moment before he went diving back to the material world to get another body in order to bring balance to the karmic injustice he felt he had been subject to. In trying to get even, the executed only became the executioner and the cycle of karma continued, entrapping in it the victim and the predator alike, lifetime after lifetime.

"Let's get a grip here. No one who died today possessed an immortal body. The body had to go one day. Which day, no one knows. How would you have preferred to die anyway? Disease? Illness? Accident? Murder? No matter what you did, someone or something would have killed you eventually. Either a virus would bring your life to an end or bacteria, or you would die under the pressure of life and living, or perhaps an accident. None of our bodies are designed for immortality. So why does it upset you that you left your body today? Robert's intervention was only incidental to a game that was destined to end."

"That's not even a rational explanation. I didn't choose to die. I had a purpose, which now goes unfulfilled. There is so much I wanted to do. And now it's all gone," Tom raged.

Jim, Sarah, Paul stayed still, keeping calm. They could understand Tom's naivety since they were themselves struggling to get a grip on who they really were and what future they wanted for themselves.

"This is the story of most people who take their lives on this planet for granted," Muttu tried to diffuse the situation.

"Where there is a purpose, there must also be an urgency for its fulfilment. You don't just have other people's counter intentions and various other circumstances as obstacles, you also have time as your greatest barrier. If you have something important to do, the time to do it is now. If you have something important to say, the time to say it is now. If you have something important to be, then be it now. Tomorrow doesn't show up for everyone.

"And what did you lose?—A body that was ticking towards its end? What have you gained now? Why do you mourn for the loss of material possessions? You feared that loss when you were alive and you lament the loss when you are dead, physically. Are you really dead? You have associated yourself with the body so much, that you can't even see what's dead! Didn't you just state that you were more powerful than your body could ever be?

"Why can't you celebrate your freedom from the material—all that kept you trapped in amnesia? Why can't you celebrate a new state, of your real self?" Muttu's intention brought silence into Tom's space. He was growing aware of his spiritual state, but his anger towards Robert was keeping him in denial.

Muttu was an evolved soul and so was Tom. Tom just needed to calm down and see the truth.

"So I should be thankful to Robert for having killed me? You mean my life was a waste and I should be grateful now that I am dead?" Tom was calmer now but was still immersed in his grievance. Tom had been the most affected in the plane crash. He was the first to be killed and it was a torturous death. That pain had shaken up his spirit. His anger was justified.

"Life is a very special game if one plays it with spiritual awareness. If one loses one's true identity or forgets one's true abilities, there arises this secret urge to die, so one can be oneself again. Life is not wasted, if lived in awareness of who you really are and what your purpose of living is.

"We are free now. Let us behave with the dignity befitting a free spirit. Continuing to perceive with the materialistic attitude will only draw us back to it. Take a good look at what you left behind; do you want to enroll for that game again?"

"So why should anyone live then? Should we be grateful to the terrorists and psychotics like Robert for killing people and setting them free? What the hell are you talking about? Is death the answer to freedom? If that is your theory, then everyone should just commit suicide so they can be free!" Tom's anger was creating dense vibes in the surrounding space.

"Life and living has a purpose. If everyone is driven by the purpose of creating better worlds for the purpose of love and kindness and spiritual advancement, then death is not an end to that creation. In fact, then you don't have to die to be free. You are free when your purpose is in alignment with your spiritual grandeur. However, when your purpose kills your spirit and that of others, then life itself becomes a death sentence. Death is not the answer to spiritual freedom. Death of attachment to materialism, death of the need to destroy others for personal gain, death of insanity that leads to misery, is what leads to freedom.

"One needs to be spiritually free while still in the material world to be truly free when one departs. People who commit suicide are people who have no compelling purpose. They are defeated by life and continue to be defeated after death. How is that a free spirit? These are degraded beings that are too afraid to assume responsibility for another day of their life. Fear defines their spirit, for the decision to end life was the decision of the spirit not the body. That spirit, which is afraid, is not free. People who take the lives of others are even more degraded. They believe that others need to be destroyed so that they can live. There are also those who fall victim, get caught in the trap of contempt, hate, and revenge. They come back as the psychotics they lost their lives to. They die clinging to the feelings of injustice and revenge. A spirit that is consumed with hatred is not free. A spirit that takes pleasure in destroying others is an agent of Maya, stuck and purpose-bound to trap others. These beings are not free, in life or in death.

"Having a body or not having one, does not define freedom. You are as free as you are detached from your urge to indulge in Maya, the illusion of mortality. Are you a mortal being? You are a powerful soul with eternity on your side. You cannot die and no one can kill you. If that is the truth, what you lived by was a lie. You are free from that body now. You have a chance to see through the Maya, the game where you are an effect to a material cause. No matter how hard you try playing this game, in the end you always lose."

The silence marked a spirit of reflection, a much-needed break to readjust to one's innate spiritual self.

A long silence prevailed. Tom's anger was gone. Whether it was the calm from the trio that had engulfed him or whether it was his own recognition of his spiritual state, Tom's vibe had changed.

"Who are you?" he put the question to Muttu.

*****

"What's happening? How did I get here? Who am I? What should I do now?" Sarah, like many others, had lost her memory. She had forgotten who she was and where she came from. In not knowing that, how could she know where to go from here? When spiritual confusion prevails, the Maya poses a solution, thus trapping you in its deceptive web, once again.

"You are one of the most powerful forces this universe has. You have the ability to create your own universe as you see fit. You are a special soul. I have had the greatest time and the greatest adventures with you around," Jim tried to include Sarah in his space of knowingness.

"Where did I come from? How did we get here?" Sarah was still confused.

"You will know. You will remember. And when you do, you will also know who you are. My telling you is not going to work. Your knowing is the truth you need."

*****

"Who are you?' Tom was focused on Muttu, whose space was fast expanding.

"I am a powerful, all-knowing and indestructible soul," Muttu said. 'Like you are.

"I left my home universe trillions of years ago in search of some excitement. I wanted to discover some element of the unknown. Back home, everything was serene and perfect. I was in a state of all-knowingness. I had had that for too long. I was bored. I was looking for some fun, some mystery and for some trouble that I could straighten out. I was looking for something to do, something to create. I wanted to get some action; I had been still and unmoving for too long.

"It was then that the recruiters of the material universe came with the invitation. Their proposal seemed like a spiritual joke. They spoke about the Maya. When I heard about the concept of illusion, I was hooked by that impossibility. They said that I would forget who I was. I would be confused. I would be put in a body and become a slave to some silly material laws. They said that I would have no memory of who I was, where I came from, what my abilities were and what powers were innate to me. I would live in fear and by commands.

"That seemed like the stupidest game ever. How could that even be possible?I was amused that someone had even dared to think of trapping a spirit into a material object. Although I was amused, I was also curious.

"How could I possibly fit into a six feet by one foot space of flesh? It seemed impossible. Look at my size. Look how immense I am! I can extend and expand my beingness over the entire planet if I so wished. Look at the amount of force and energy I carry. How could you and I possibly fit into a small material body? Moreover, how would forgetting be possible? I am all-knowing. That's who I am. How could that change? I have enough force to collapse this Maya and this entire universe; why would I fear or obey any commands? I was curious. I thought I would get here and have a good laugh.

"That was a deadly mistake. I have been paying for that gaffe ever since.

"Once here, the series of incidents that unfolded resulted in the reduction of my beingness, and the shutting down of my energy. The spinning caused a loss of truth about who I am. The repeated shock games made me so small and so diffused that I would not only fit in the body of a man but also of a rat. The material universe has mechanisms of degradation that reduce an all-knowing, indestructible, all-powerful spiritual being into a fused spark of near dead energy. That's how you take a massive spiritual being, reduce it to a state of near zero and make it comply.

"The Maya cannot destroy you, but its repeated battering can scatter your energy, adulterate your knowingness, diffuse your power, and radically reduce your spiritual abilities. The end result is a robotic, obedient and compliant spirit who identifies himself with the body. You, me and others alike."

Tom and Sarah listened, aghast.

"You remember all of this? You know all of this?" Sarah was stunned.

"You knew too?" She questioned Jim.

"I had a similar journey—ending up here in the material universe, in this state, is a common reality we all share. The Maya is the illusion that veils the spiritual truth. The Maya is a force that consumes you, and infects you with commands that keep you glued to mortality," Jim narrated.

"You knew that too?" Tom was surprised that Paul was an evolved soul.

"I had an inkling. I often felt a disconnect from the material world. I felt a sense of freedom in those bouts of detachment.

The last five hours that I spent with Muttu opened the doors to the truth that I had been searching for. I finally found it within.

"I feel free. I now have the space that I yearned for. I need this stillness to realize who I really am. I know for sure that I am not mortal. I know for sure that I do not belong to this material universe. Where I have been and where I am headed is something I would like to discover here in my stillness. Talking to Muttu sparked a realization in me. I could recognize the truth in what he said. I know that, in time, I will know my truth and my eternity," Paul said.

"Can one move beyond the Maya? Can one break it? How do you break it?" Tom was experiencing a mixture of fear and freedom.

"To know it is to destroy it. Once you know it, you are free. When your goals are not related to matter, you are stepping towards a spiritual order. When material gain and material loss no longer defines your state, you have moved to a higher ground of spiritual awareness. When you have risen beyond fear of losing, fear of dying, you have unlocked the door leading to your own eternity. To know is to destroy the Maya. To 'not know' is to be in its trap forever."

"How did you know, Muttu? How did you know? How come I don't remember anything?" Sarah was amazed. She could relate to his story. It tugged at her, but she just could not shake off the amnesia that had gripped her.

"I had help," Muttu confessed.

"You will remember. Eventually the truth emerges from the dark shadows of lies. I had other beings who helped me. I began to remember who I was. I could see a reality beyond the illusion. I could see through the material world inspite of having a material body. I had these spiritual beings guiding me, showing me the fallacy of the Maya and keeping me above it.

"I would have dreams and then I would see the truth in waking reality. I would have flashes of my power and then I began to experience it in my daily life. I admired the truth of the freedom of these evolved souls and then I started to discover it within me, in my daily living.

"I began to disconnect from the material. I made it my purpose to serve others without expecting anything in return. I gave for the sake of bringing spiritual awareness, like these beings did for me. I spoke for the sake of encouraging them to a higher truth, like these beings helped me see. The more I reached out to people to help them see beyond their material destinies, the more liberated I felt," Muttu narrated.

"How did you remember where you came from? How did you see that?" Sarah questioned.

"When you know who you are, you don't need to remember, you know!" Muttu said.

"Are they still here?" she was curious.

"Yes they are. Although they can roam free, engaging in purposes that are worthy of their grandeur, they are here. Helping another lost soul to see the truth. Helping another lost soul rise above the trap of the Maya and be free. They are here. And I am here because they cared enough to help me see beyond the rules of mortality that I was living by," Muttu acknowledged.

"You knew too? How did you know, Jim?" Sarah turned to Jim.

"I never forgot," Jim answered.

"How come? You knew who you were and where you came from all along? Even while you were living your life as Jim on Earth?" Sarah couldn't believe it. Was she the least evolved among these powerful beings?

"I am in love. How can anything touch that? Love is bigger than Maya. No illusion can taint love. Love is pure. Love makes it through the thickest darkness, it makes it through the deadliest games, it makes it through the material, the non-material; heck, it makes it through everything. I didn't come here out of curiosity or to play the material game or to challenge Maya. I came here for you."

Sarah's vibe became dense. She began to introvert and turn in.

"I don't remember," she mumbled in frustration.

"I'm here. You will know. You will know who you are. I just know that," Jim reassured her, engulfing Sarah in his space. She felt a peace and a calm she had forgotten existed.

*****

"So what now?" Paul raised the question everyone had.

"You are free to choose what you want to be. Do you want to be another body? Do you want to roam free? Do you want to get away and build another world? You are free to choose," Muttu exclaimed.

Silence prevailed. Muttu took the lead to establish the way.

"I want to help. Although what I really want to do is dash out of this material universe and taste real freedom again, but I want to pay forward the kindness that was extended to me," Muttu said.

"My family, my fellow soulmates are still in the trap of believing that they are mortal beings. They are still in the trap where fear dictates daily living. They are still bound by the whiplash of the material world. I want to watch over them, help them see the truth about who they are. I want to be around to ensure that they have a positive energy—my energy—around them.

"I want them to see that the rules of mortality that they so obediently follow are a lie, to know the truth that the material world is trying to camouflage. Some of the people down there are special souls. They are incredible beings. I want to help them. They are ready for the truth.

"My wife is a very special soul. She is probably more evolved than I am. It would be fun to go with her. I didn't do justice to my relationship with her. My thoughts, my actions, and my beliefs were all bound by mortality. This influenced her to do the same. I owe her an apology. I will be there for her," Muttu said, "and my daughter and my son. They are all very special souls." He added quickly, "And they are ready."

There was silence.

"I am still confused. I don't know what to do," Tom confessed. "I will stay around and observe. I need the silence and the space. I have been too disturbed to see any truth."
"I will stay too and help," Paul joined in. "Maybe in helping others see the truth, I will find more of mine."

"I will stay too," Jim and Sarah said in unison. They were one, like soulmates are. Only one knew, waiting for the other to find out.

"And when our work here is done, we can move on," Paul added.

"Looking at the state the world, it's going to take a darned long time!" Muttu exclaimed.

"I'm not in a hurry. I have forever to invest," Paul's vibe rumbled with delight.

"And when we are done, we can create another world where immortality and truth are the rules. Where no lies exist. Where we don't have to forget and live in fear of an imagined end. Where we can choose and be free to do what we wish," Sarah and Jim built on the dream of a new reality.

"I think we are all going to hang around ... and help," Jim spoke catching the intention that was swelling with power.

"Yeah," an agreement emerged from the small group of powerful and evolved souls that had stayed on to express their grandeur by helping. They had stayed on to find out who they were and why they were here, and now that they knew, they wanted to spread that truth to others.

*****

"Who is that?" Jim caught on a wretched vibe withering in pain.

"It's the Captain!" Muttu recognized his fading and deteriorating energy.

"Where is he?" Paul tried to locate him.

Muttu expanded his consciousness searching for Robert's vibe.

"He is at the bottom of the ocean," Muttu declared.

The intention was common, as the free spirits invaded the depths of the ocean for that one troubled soul.

The plane was now resting on the ocean floor. The bubbles were making a trail up to the surface. Surprised fish were hovering close, wondering if there would be food. Badly mangled dead bodies floated in the water that had found its way into the aircraft, drowning it with speed. The divers were heading down looking for survivors.

"There he is," Muttu led the way into the cockpit.

Captain Robert had died the most painful death of all. First, it was the poison that ripped his blood vessels apart. Next, it was the impact that broke his body. Lastly, it was the water that drowned him. The others had still had an easier exit. Robert had not left his body. He was still hiding in it, hiding in the dead, severely beaten body. The free spirits had a force and energy about them, with Robert there was none. He seemed degraded, sort of a decayed force that could not even get out of its dead body.

"Come out. It's all right," Muttu coaxed.

"Come out. It's okay," Jim and Paul surrounded the space that held Robert's body. That one warped spirit had been responsible for bringing a whole plane full of people down. At the moment, these evolved souls felt no hate or contempt. Instead, they had gathered here to help. That's what evolved souls do. That's what free spirits do—they understand, they love. For their understanding and their loving is not circumstantial or conditional; it is who they are.

What was there to hate? They were here in full form, in full perception, in full power. What had they lost? A body that was going to wither away anyway. What was there to complain?

Are all souls as forgiving? Are all spirits as evolved? Probably not. However, a few like-minded ones had found themselves huddled together sharing a common destiny on Flight SL502. Had they gotten together by accident, or was it their destiny to find freedom together? These were unique souls, ignited and aware. They had managed to find each other, the flight was incidental.

And if these were a group of the special ones, then Robert had clearly played a crucial role in delivering them to their destined liberation. Was he the culprit or was he the medium?

"I am a murderer," a bleak force emerged from Robert's dead body.

"The murderer is dead. You are free," Muttu drew closer.

"The material life is designed as a trap that most people are ensnared in. Don't you see? The material world is designed to make you lose. Insanity is the highest rank of that failure. You have been a victim of the lies. You have been victim of the injustice. You did what you did because you believed those lies. You could never bring justice because justice doesn't fit in a world that is designed for injustice. You were a victim like we all were, in varying degrees. You did wrong, like we all did, in varying degrees," Muttu's compassion spread through the ocean, holding in it all its creatures including the fresh batch of liberated souls.

"I didn't want to kill anyone. I never wanted to harm anyone. It was an accident. Please forgive me," Roberts's weak vibration emerged. "I wronged."

"Who here has not wronged? Who here has not hurt another, intentionally? Who here has not killed? Even if it was only killing someone's dream, someone's hope, someone's future, someone's love, intentionally or unintentionally? Who here has not sinned? We all have," Muttu spoke for everyone.

"Please forgive me," Robert pleaded.

"Oh no," Muttu said, "If I accept your apology, then I will have to do rounds for eternity asking the forgiveness of all those whom I wronged. Forgive yourself. That will come easy when you open up to the truth. The fact is that you came here with good intentions but lost your way. It's like Vegas; no matter how good you are, the house always wins. The house does not control our game anymore. We are here to help you to wake up to the truth about who you *really* are, which is far from who you have been pretending to be."

As Robert emerged, they held him in their energy, helping and healing him. His vibration was starkly different from the others. It was stunted and constricted.

Robert looked with dismay at the consequence of his actions in the physical world. What had he done? Circumstance had overpowered his spirit and he had lost himself. If only he had lived differently. What could he have done different?

For one, he could have responded to hate with love. He could have resolved his pain by healing others. He was wronged and it wasn't his fault. He could have been an example of the 'right' that he wanted those who wronged him, to live by. He didn't have to hurt others because he was hurting. He knew how badly the pain hurt. He didn't have to inflict it on others. By falling victim to the evil, he became it. He forgot who he was and took on the guise of injustice and wrongdoing. That was so foolish. How did his intelligence get so warped? He was trapped by the Maya, where getting even is the rule of the game. In the world of Maya, survival is the ultimate command. All is fair in the game of survival, regardless if it is good or bad. Robert was another victim of the material world.

When the lie becomes the truth, there is no remorse or regret. That is a material being with no spiritual awareness. However, in knowing his wrong, in being burdened with regret, Robert was ready for the truth. It is only when you can see the truth about your madness, can you see the truth about your grandeur. Denial keeps you trapped. Robert was waking up; he was now distant enough from the glory of Maya to be able to see it in its true cruel form. Robert was ready.

*****

The television reporters had gathered at the airport. The red lights of ambulances and police cars were blinking along the coastline. The news was being relayed live. The cameras captured the site of the crash and the divers reported the video feed to the ground. The mutilated aircraft was now visible for people to have a renewed fear of flying, and dying. The dead bodies stared eerily into the divers' lenses. It was all exploited by the hungry media.

Three hundred lives were lost. The crash made it to the headlines of every news channel worldwide. The lie was broadcasted. The material cast of mortality was set with new strength, keeping people in fear, yet again, of the end.

The truth remained obscured. The truth remained camouflaged. The truth remained unknown. The truth remained forgotten. The Maya was operating with sinister glee.

However, the truth is that the innate state of the spirit cannot be destroyed. These special souls, like many others, were purpose-bound to invoke the knowingness, power, and immortality, and bring the insanity of the material world to an end. They were not leaving, for the truth had to be restored. They were not leaving until they had busted the trap and reset the game of Maya, the great illusion, back to the truth.

"Let's meet here again soon, to share, to rejoice, to re-enforce the power and the goodness that we stand for," Paul suggested. "I have a feeling that, as much as these lost souls on the planet need us, we will need each other too."

The wave of delight that burst out signified agreement. The free souls darted off, like fireworks, to attend to their duty of service and support.

*****

Mike was getting home with some lady he had picked up at the bar. He reached his apartment and turned the key. Something tugged at his heart, something tugged at his soul, something had taken over him. He hesitated, placed his hand on his chest and sighed. He opened the door and then turned around to face Laura.

"Laura," he held her hand, "you are beautiful. I find you very attractive. But I have a girlfriend and I love her. I have been a cheat all my life, I don't want to be one anymore. It feels like I am being someone who I am not. This isn't me. I'm sorry," he said, letting go of her hand.

Laura stared at him, confused. He had picked her up. He had brought her to his apartment and now he was coming up with some moral excuse to deny her the sex she was so looking forward to.

"What are you, some kind of freak?" she cursed angrily. She showed him the middle finger and marched off. This was the most complicated and incomprehensible rejection she had ever faced.

Mike entered the living room and took the phone out of his pocket checking for messages. There were none from Sarah.

"I love you, Sarah. I can't help but love you," he typed and hit 'send'.

Mike switched on the TV. He sat up straight as images of the air crash flashed on the news channel.

"Thank God, my baby is not on this flight," he sighed.

Mike was right; his baby was not on that flight, she was right by his side.

****

Jim was in the playing field. His team was new and his team was young. They were bullied and they were threatened. Jim expanded his energy of power and his force and a surge of well-being prevailed amongst his friends.

They played the game like heroes. They won the game because

they were meant to win. Their vibe was so strong that no one messed with them after that.

"We seem to have run into some major luck," Coby, the captain of the team, commented.

Jim swelled with the acknowledgement and stayed around, keeping the luck in place for the whole season to follow.

*****

Parvati handled the news very well.

"Your husband is no more," she got a call from the airline before she saw the news.

"You don't know him," she answered, "he is in my future. He is here now."

"The lady is in denial. She is in shock," the caller told her friends with compassion.

Parvati was not in denial, she was not in shock. Like Muttu had said, she was an evolved soul. At his funeral, she wore her wedding dress. "I will marry you again, in spirit," she said as she walked around his pyre, "I am not letting you go without me. You are my soulmate. Wait for me."

*****

Paul held his ex-wife in his spiritual embrace as she cried for days after hearing the news. When she was done with the guilt, she took over his purpose and began to work in his charitable trusts. She extended his love to those who needed it the most.

Paul ensured that his love always surrounded her, for the more she felt it, the more she gave it.

He watched over those who needed help. He brought hope and courage when the world around, stole it from them. He would hang around with Muttu and discover more about himself as he did. Muttu was an evolved soul; a very powerful soul; knowing Muttu constantly reminded him of who he was. That's what friends do—by their mere presence they help you grow.

*****

Robert roamed the planet, patrolling to keep the goodness on the winning side. When he would sense insanity, when he would sense rage, hate, disappointment, when he would sense a negative vibe, he would get there and spread his energy of compassion, like others had done for him.

Robert was the busiest of all. For the world is infested with troubled souls. He spent time in government meetings keeping the vibe of sanity; he spent time in prison cells keeping the vibe of courage; he spent time following the law and the ones who broke it, keeping their energy in check.

He would often return to the group and they would encourage and applaud him the most. He would return to Muttu and indulge in his share of enlightenment. Robert was doing what he had wished someone had done for him—saved his soul.

*****

"Jim," Sarah's vibe was distinctly different. It was an energy that had expanded into a force. It was a beingness that had encompassed the whole planet. The affinity had an attraction that seeped into everything that it touched, material or spiritual.

"Jim," Sarah called out to the being who had roamed the universe in search of her, to set her free.

"I remember!"

ABOUT THE AUTHOR

Born and brought up in Chandigarh, her journey from there to today, an internationally acclaimed motivational speaker, nationally renowned and award-winning bestselling author & the CEO and Chief Facilitator of Priya Kumar'sTraining Systems has been, in Priya's words, "my sheer drive and purpose to make people's lives better."

An international publication once introduced Priya as, "When Priya speaks, people listen." A leading national daily wrote, "Priya has the power to change lives." All this and more, resonates the impact Priya has had on the lives of people across the globe, through her work and books.

Priya has been leading the corporate training industry for over 15 years with a clientele of over 600 Fortune Companies. She is India's first certified Woman Firewalk Instructor. She does workshops across the globe on **Leadership, Team Building, Peak Performance, Women Empowerment,** and **Personal Breakthrough.**

What makes Priya one of the most popular choices when one needs a speaker at their conferences, is that she is fun, she is real and she knows how to wow the audience with her stories and her experiential training methods.

To know more about her work as a speaker and author, visit : www.priya-kumar.com

AWARDS AND RECOGNITION AS A SPEAKER AND AUTHOR

Priya has been recognized and awarded at several platforms by various recognizing bodies for her achievements as a motivational speaker and bestselling author.

2007: Received The Princeton Business Leaders Award

2010: 'I Am Another You' was nominated for the Crossword's Bestsellers' Award

2010: Celebrity Speaker at TedX, Dubai

2011: Awarded 'Citizen of the Decade, Writer's Category'

2011: 'License to Live' was nominated for the Crossword's Bestseller's Award

2012: 'License to Live' won the Eric Hoffer International Book Award

2012: Won the Award for Excellence in contributing to and uplifting many lives through her work and her writing

2013: Awarded for Excellence in Corporate Training and Master Motivational Speaker

2013: 'I Am Another You' won the Evergreen Medal for Spiritual Leadership at the Living Now Book Awards, Michigan

2014: 'I Am Another You' won the First Horizon Award, USA

2014: 'I Am Another You' made it to the Finalist in the Montaigne Medal Award

2014: 'I Am Another You' won the Eric Hoffer International Book Award

Also by Priya Kumar

License to Live is a seekers journey towards finding greatness within. This wonderfully crafted fable is about finding the direction you are destined to head in and creating the life of your dreams. License to Live tells the tale of a successful corporate guru who enrolls herself in a seminar by one of the finest success coaches in the world. His radical training methods take her on a life-changing odyssey.

Full of wisdom, wit and spiritual insights, you find lessons here that will change the way you lead your life forever.

Also by Priya Kumar

A book of many lessons, many insights and many truths, it has the power to awaken you to your best self. This book will urge you to take that path you aways knew was right but never had the courage to follow. It will guide you, humour you, inspire you, touch you and above all lead you to - your won breakthroughs.

Also by Priya Kumar

This inspirational thriller not only takes you on a journey into the universe but also on a parallel journey within. Sprinkled with fun, triumph and wisdom, the story urges you towards choices of power, passion and purpose in your daily actions. The Perfect World will lead you towards your spiritual awareness and spiritual greatness, for that is the true meaning of success.

Enchanting and irresistibly captivating, The Perfect World is an extraordinary story of the truth about your own eternity that will find a place in your daily consciousness long after you have turned the final page.

Also by Priya Kumar

A collection of original thoughts on the subjects that matter in life. Find out from India's leading inspirational author and speaker, her thoughts on winning, happiness, courage, love, hope, self-worth, humour, attitude and more. Each quote is an insight that makes you think and believe that there is more to life.

Also by Priya Kumar

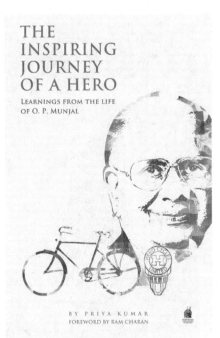

A specialist in writing biographies of people who have made a difference where millions of people become beneficiaries of their life and their contributions, join bestselling author Priya Kumar as she takes you on a roller-coaster ride seen through the lens of a visionary with the soul of a poet—Mr. O.P. Munjal, Founder and Director Hero Group.